The Couple in Cabin 2124

A Patricia Fisher Mystery

Book 4

Steve Higgs

Dedication

To Mary Kelsey for creating Edgar and Erica Brentnall

Table of Contents:

An Evening Stroll Ruined

The sun slowly set over the port quarter of the ship's nose as I took a quiet walk around the ship. I did this most nights before retiring with a book. It helped me order my thoughts and commit to memory as many of the wonderful things I had seen and experienced as possible. It was the height of summer now and I was almost halfway through my cruise around the world, a fact which both pleased and saddened at the same time.

That I had been able to take this trip in the first place ought to be a sore subject, but it wasn't. My husband cheated on me and my flight from that situation led me to take up residence in the Royal Suite of the world's finest luxury cruise ship. Since then, my life had become a whirlwind of adventure, exotic places and incredible experiences. The only element I could possibly be unhappy about was having no one to share it with. Our marriage was into its thirty-third year when the cheating took place. Or rather, that was when I caught him cheating. Walking down the aisle at just nineteen when I met *the one* and was happily swept off my feet, I never considered that the moonlight and sparkles might one day lose their shine. They did though and three decades later, the vibrant young girl I had been was buried beneath the shroud of a middle-aged woman with no particular purpose and no perceptible joy.

The ship was currently bound for Japan where it would dock in Tokyo for two days. The passage from Hawaii was the second longest of the trip, unavoidably, because there was nothing between Hawaii and Japan apart from a vast expanse of Pacific Ocean. Now, almost exactly four days into that leg, I was ready to get off and explore again when we docked tomorrow morning. I had a niggling concern that my estranged husband might show up, but every time the thought raised its head, I knocked it back down with a derisory laugh. Charlie never went anywhere. It was a fact that had angered me for most of our marriage but was now something I could rely on. A week ago, he called me in my cabin and promised to meet me in Hawaii. He hadn't showed of course, but the niggling doubt remained because, despite years of avoiding planes and travel, he had been waiting for me in St Kitts when the ship docked there. I avoided him then, leaving him on the quayside even though I knew he was coming and had agreed to meet with him to discuss our future. He went home, but not until after he expressed his displeasure at wasting his time. Now I wasn't sure what he might do.

There was one thing I was sure about: I had moved on. The forced time apart allowed me to shrug off the shroud and rediscover myself hiding beneath it. The vibrancy returned almost overnight, so I now felt excited each morning by the prospect of the day ahead.

Then there was the captain to consider.

I didn't get to focus my thoughts on Captain Alistair Huntley's handsome features though, because I reached the stern of the enormous ship, I came across a sight that cleared my mind of everything else: there was a man climbing over the railings.

'Hey,' I called out. Then again louder, 'Hey!' as I continued to walk toward him. I looked around but there was no one else about. It was late, so the passengers would be in bars or restaurants or in the many theatres, cinemas or clubs the great ship boasted. It was probably why the man chose this time to come up here and the feeling of dread telling me he was on his way to commit suicide became a definite when I saw the weight he was carrying in one hand.

I dashed to the railing at the very back of the ship, but unwilling to climb over as he had, I tried calling yet again. This time he heard me and turned his head revealing the mask of pain on his face. It broke my heart instantly and I wondered what I could possibly say that might convince him to reconsider. I didn't have to present an argument for life though because he instantly started back toward me.

Beyond the railing at the very back of the ship, were steel mesh panels reaching upward to a height of around three yards and the same panels extended outwards supported on steel girders so the man was currently walking on them directly above the maelstrom of water being churned up by the ship's propellers.

I didn't know, but it was my assumption that the mesh panels were there to provide some kind of maintenance access to something. However, I was fairly certain they were not meant to be accessed while at sea. Despite the man's mask of misery, he made his way back from the edge to the other side of the mesh separating us. My heart was thumping in my chest but beginning to calm down. That was until he stopped. I expected him to start climbing; to be depressed enough about his life to contemplate suicide but to have changed his mind the moment he saw someone take an interest.

Instead, he dug around in a pocket to pull out a small folded note, then he grabbed the mesh, his fingers curling through it right next to where I was also holding it so that his skin touched mine in several places. 'You're Patricia Fisher, aren't you?' he said. It was a question, but I felt that he already knew the answer before I nodded. He looked up to the sky at that point as if having an argument with God.

When he looked back down, I said, 'Please come back onto the ship. It's not safe out there. You don't want to do this.' The weight I spotted earlier was tied around his waist with a belt. It was a round disc that he must have taken from one of the gyms and looked to weigh fifty pounds or more. With it tied to him, he would sink like a rock if he jumped.

3

The man looked squarely at me as he replied, 'It's too late for me.'

'No, it isn't,' I pleaded, trying to get through to him. 'We can work through this.'

He just shook his head. Then he thrust the note through the mesh and into my hand as he yelled, 'You have to save Anna. Nothing else matters. I've caused too much harm already. I jump now or they kill me tomorrow.' I stared blankly at his face, trying to think of something I could say, but nothing came. 'Save Anna!' he yelled once more. Then he let go of the railing, turned and started running.

A panicked gasp escaped my lips as fear for what I was about to see filled my belly. I screamed, 'No!' at his back and had to watch as he reached the end of the platform and jumped; the weight held in his hands and against his body as he dropped. I don't think my heart bothered to beat in the time it took for him to fall and hit the churning surf below. Then he was gone. Gone forever, swallowed by the restless waves as, unknowingly, the ship continued onwards to its destination.

I heaved in ragged gulps of air as I continued to stare at the spot where he entered the water. I knew of course, that had he somehow bobbed back to the surface, he would have been hundreds of yards behind the ship already as it thrust itself forward at close to forty knots, but I couldn't take my eyes off the waves.

When my heartrate finally started to slow, I looked about again but there was still no one in sight. What I did spot though was a man-over-board alarm. It was a large red button with an even larger red sign above it. I knew there was nothing anyone could do for the man, but I pressed it anyway and then slumped to the cold deck to wait for the ship's security team to arrive.

Thinking back to it later, I had to commend the crew for their response time. I hadn't timed it, of course, but the sound of footsteps must have first reached my ears no more than sixty seconds after pushing the alarm button. There was no audible claxon, probably to avoid startling guests, many of whom were elderly and might not do well with the shock. It had to have alerted the crew in another way though because dozens of them appeared.

When I asked Lieutenant Baker about it, one of the ship's security I had come to know quite well, he said the alarm sounded inside the bridge and showed them which alarm button had been pushed. That set in motion a series of actions, the first of which was to put out a call to every member of crew with a radio, dispatching them to the location.

Lieutenant Baker was not the first to arrive, but he was the first familiar face and I was glad to speak with someone I knew. All I had managed to stammer at the first person was, 'He jumped,' as I pointed from my position on the deck toward the stern of the ship. The first person was a female member of the ship's security team. Her immediate reaction was to run where I pointed and stare fruitlessly into the murky water. When, seconds later, the next person arrived, they joined her as did the next and the next.

One of the actions enacted by the bridge was an immediate shut down of the engines. To their minds, there could be a person, passenger or crew, in the water and they had a very small window to respond before that person was lost forever. At the speed the ship travelled, anyone going overboard would be left in its wake, a tiny dot that would vanish from sight and never be found unless the crew reacted fast enough.

I knew how futile their efforts were though.

'Are you alright, Mrs Fisher?' asked Lieutenant Baker as he returned from the stern and knelt next to me.

I looked up at him with a grim smile. 'He jumped,' I said again. It was like my brain was caught in a loop and couldn't come up with any other response.

Baker leaned in closer, using a hand to steady himself against the cold deck as he crouched. 'Who did? Who jumped, Mrs Fisher?'

I just shrugged. I had no idea who the man had been. At the back of the ship, by the railings, someone shouted that they might have seen something, and all eyes trained on where they were pointing. I snapped out of my reverie, Baker offering his hand to help me up as I began clambering to my feet. 'You can't save him,' I shouted loud enough for everyone to hear.

'Why not?' asked Commander Shriver. I hadn't seen the tall, thin woman arrive, but she was joining the crew members at the stern now, the question coming over her shoulder as she walked.

I was on my feet now, so I joined her, addressing the ship's stand-in Deputy Captain when I said, 'He had a weight tied to his waist. A heavy-looking plate for a barbell in the gym,' I explained. 'He sank instantly.'

'Do you know who it was?' she asked, taking the news that someone had committed suicide in her stride.

I shook my head no. 'I was taking a walk when I spotted him going over the top of the railings. He wasn't someone I recognised.'

She took a moment to absorb what I had told her, then asked another question. 'Did he say anything at all?'

I swallowed hard against the unwarranted feeling of guilt now rising in my gut and searched my memory to recall his final words. I stared at nothing for a second, then refocused my eyes on her face. 'He said, "It's too late for me. I jump now or they kill me tomorrow." Then he ran and leapt. I watched him all the way down.'

Then she asked, 'Do you remember anything else about him? His age, his accent, anything about his features?'

I described him as best as I could, the fleeting memory not filled with detail as I had been too focused on the impending horror to take much in. Doing the best that I could, I provided them with the details of a Japanese man who was six feet tall or thereabouts, late thirties with jet-black hair shot through with grey around his temples. His nose wasn't completely straight, though not so distorted that he looked like an old and broken boxer. He wore a wedding ring, I remembered seeing it glint when he put his fingers through the railings, and his English was impeccable though heavily accented to make me believe he was not only Japanese, but also from Japan rather than from somewhere else in the world.

Commander Shriver wriggled her nose in thought before speaking into her lapel microphone. She turned away but I could still hear that she was reporting to the captain. I heard her say my name and listened to it cause the voice at the other end to pause. I even heard his response when he said, 'Of course Mrs Fisher is there. Who else could it have been?' I didn't want to read too much into it, but it sounded like he was annoyed to hear I was involved.

At my side, Baker said, 'There's nothing more you can do here, Mrs Fisher. The ship has been set to stop so that launches can be dispatched to search the area the person entered the water. This is something we practise, and we have to go through the entire drill even though I am sure you are right, and he is not able to be saved.' He looked into my eyes, checking that I was okay. 'Can I have you escorted back to your suite, Mrs Fisher?'

I looked to the sky and breathed in deeply before I replied. 'Thank you, Lieutenant Baker. I will make my own way home.' With that I touched him on the shoulder, turned and began back along the deck toward my suite located all the way down at the front of the giant ship.

I don't know how long it took for me to get there, but nothing registered as I made my way from the stern of the ship to the door of the Windsor Suite. My brain insisted on replaying the man's final words over and over as it supplied a remembered image of his body entering the cruel sea and vanishing forever.

Fumbling in my bag for my keycard, my hand came across a piece of paper. It was what the man had thrust into my hand right before he begged me to save Anna. I had completely forgotten it. Standing outside my door, I unfolded the piece of paper to look at it. There were some odd lines on the outside that were supposed to be a pattern or something. It didn't look like anything to me, so I turned it over. On the other side was the number 2124. I held it up to the light but there was nothing else to see, just some squiggly lines and a cabin number. In the man's final moments, the desperately unhappy man had entrusted me with a clue to help me find and save Anna and it was as mysterious and cryptic as it could possibly be.

I checked my watch. It was getting late and already after my usual bedtime, but I knew I wouldn't sleep so there was little point in trying. I also knew my butler, Jermaine, would be waiting inside my suite for me to safely return before he would consider retiring to bed himself. With a grimace of acceptance, I swiped my keycard on the door and let myself in, calling out as I came through the door to get his attention, 'Jermaine.'

'Yes, madam,' he answered, appearing at the entrance from the lobby to the living area half a heartbeat later as if hovering there while he waited for my return. He probably had been.

'Jermaine, something terrible happened.' As his expression instantly filled with concern, I walked him into my living area and insisted he take a seat on one of the couches so I could explain about the suicide, the man's last words and the note. He listened intently, nodding but not saying anything. 'I think this is a cabin number,' I said, showing him the piece of paper. 'I need to see who is staying in this cabin.'

'Very good, madam,' replied Jermaine, rising to his feet to cross the room. I knew that he could obtain the names of the passengers in the room from central registry, the information with us in a second. The names didn't mean anything though. Not to me at least, though they had clearly meant something to the man who jumped. Erica and Edgar Brentnall, a British couple that boarded the ship in Southampton on the same day as me and were due to leave the ship when it returned to Southampton. Another around the world trip.

'Where is cabin 2124?' I asked.

Jermaine's eyes flicked up and right as he scoured his memory for the information, no doubt cross-referencing a map of the ship's layout in his head. 'That is deck eight and I think it is inboard so one of the smaller cabins with no porthole to outside. It should be roughly midships, I think.'

It was way down in the bowels of the ship, one deck above the bottom deck for passengers. The six decks below that were all reserved for crew, storage, engineering, laundry etcetera and it was located in one of the inside passageways. In order to accommodate so many passengers and to provide for a range of budgets, there were many cabins that were significantly smaller and less desirable than others. That I was staying in the most opulent suite on board the ship was not something I would ever bring up in conversation. It wasn't as if I could actually afford it. Had I not been the subject of a plan to steal a priceless jewel and leave me framed for murder, I would most likely have left the ship and returned to England already, getting back as much of my money as I could in the process. As it was, my trip was free all bar the travelling expenses I incurred for food and drink and whatever I spent ashore and in the shops on board.

I looked at the clock again and made a decision. Jermaine asked, 'Are you going out, madam?' sounding a little surprised.

I had my handbag over my left arm, and I was heading for the door. 'I want to see the cabin,' I replied. 'This man died before anyone could help him and he asked me to save Anna. I haven't the slightest idea what is going on or who Anna is or even how the couple in cabin 2124 are involved but I intend to find out.'

Jermaine coughed politely to attract my attention. 'Madam, I feel aggrieved to remind you. But you did promise the captain that you would avoid any further sleuthing while on board.' He genuinely looked embarrassed to make the point, recognising perhaps that it was not his place to do so. He was right though; I had made that promise.

His gentle cough caused my feet to stop moving, but they started again now, onward toward the door. 'This isn't sleuthing, Jermaine,' I called over my shoulder. 'This is poking my nose in and that's entirely different.'

I heard him sigh and caught a glimpse of his eye roll as I reached the lobby and glanced back to see what he was doing. He was following me, of course, accompanying the mad woman as she set off on another quest.

It was late enough that the lights in the passageways had been dimmed. The ship went into night-time routine much like the streets at home, but it was not so late that the passageways were empty. A lot of the passengers were only on board for a short leg, a few days in some cases, so the constant churn of new people ensured the party atmosphere never diminished. The clubs, bars, restaurants, theatres, and cinemas were generally packed with young and old excited to have a good time. It was one of the elements of my time on board that I hadn't been able to fully enjoy. Not really. Travelling alone meant I made friends, but they were gone all too soon and most of the friends I did make either already had their own friends with them; there were lots of widows travelling in twos and threes, or they were with a partner.

Anyway, there were lots of people about and I figured there was a good chance that the couple in cabin 2124 would be out at this time but on their way back to their cabin soon. I would be right or wrong, so if they were already inside, my time and Jermaine's would be wasted. I wasn't going to knock on their door, but if they were out and heading back soon, there was a chance to see them or hear them and that, I felt, was worth investing a little time in.

The vast dimensions of the ship usually meant that getting anywhere on foot took ages. Barbie, one of the ship's fitness instructors and, along with Jermaine, a friend who I inevitably involved in my adventures, had a cabin in the staff area below deck seven. To get there could take more than thirty minutes. Of course, size zero, super fit Barbie ran the journey each time, so it probably took less than ten minutes on her young legs, but getting to cabin 2124 was a cinch.

The nearest elevator to my suite on the upper deck was less than one hundred yards away and it took us all the way down to the eighth deck without stopping once for people to get on and off. Then, I discovered that the cabin I wanted was again less than one hundred yards from the elevator again.

It was Jermaine's expert knowledge of the ship that located it so quickly, but then I was faced with what to do next. My butler and I were standing in a passageway, aimlessly staring at nothing because there was nothing to look at. On the upper decks the walls between the cabin doors were adorned with paintings, some of them quite ornate and expensive. This far down in the ship, there wasn't much decoration other than safety posters.

Rather than hang around in the passageway, where we looked particularly out of place, we retreated back to the elevators where hanging about looked less suspicious. Jermaine took up a sentry like position close to the elevator bank, bowed his head and waited patiently like he was a ninja in meditation mode. I didn't have the same ability to distance myself or centre my core or whatever it was he was doing, so I fidgeted and picked at my nails and tried to distract myself by mentally reciting all the Charles Dickens books and Shakespeare sonnets. After what felt like an eternity, I turned to Jermaine and asked, 'How long have we been waiting?'

My butler cracked open just one eye, calmly pulled his pocket watch from its hiding place in his waistcoat and replied, 'Three minutes, twelve seconds, madam.'

I knew time always moved more slowly when there was nothing to do, but this was silly. Blowing out an exasperated breath, I stomped back along the passageway to try their door. Jermaine shot me a concerned look as I grabbed the handle. It was locked though, the red light on the keycard panel telling me I ought not to be able to gain entry.

Then, behind Jermaine, the lift pinged, and the doors began to open. He stepped to one side but not before I quickly darted myself away from the Brentnall's door and slowed to resume a normal, innocent walking pace, checking my phone so that I seemed engrossed in that and not in anything else.

The passageways on this deck were far tighter than I was used to so the persons exiting the elevator would not be able to pass me without both parties moving to hug the wall. I looked up as they neared, pausing to take in their faces though I had no reason to believe the two people coming my way would prove to be my quarry.

They were though. The woman had a keycard in her hand which she used to swipe the panel outside 2124. I watched as they went inside, and the door closed loudly behind them. I left my suite because I was curious to see what the couple in 2124 looked like and because the poor man who leapt to his death fingered them as somehow responsible. That he couldn't have given me more detail was bothersome, but having seen them, I was certain they were to blame.

The woman was in her late thirties and stank predominantly of cigarettes as she passed me in the passageway. She had tattoos visible on the exposed flesh on her shoulders and on her neck. Her head was shaved on her left side, with the rest of it slicked over to the right. It was dyed jet black but had bright red highlights woven through it. Her clothing was a mishmash of styles; red fishnet stockings and black Doctor Martins boots below a summer dress. She had about fifteen earrings around the perimeter of the one ear I caught sight of. I wasn't one for judging other people, but she looked unpleasant.

With her was a giant bear of a man. Dressed like a biker in black tasselled leather and denim, he had to be close to six feet eight inches tall and he was big in every direction. His wide shoulders and barrel like chest, which might once have been muscular, tiered into a beer gut now. Both of them had to be at least a hundred pounds overweight, a struggle I sympathised with as I had fought my own battles with the scales over the years. Like his wife, the man also bore tattoos and stank of cigarettes and both were quite inebriated.

Jermaine moved to stand beside me, his looming presence making me feel protected and safe if nothing else. Unfortunately, it was probably the feeling of safety that caused my next move.

I had been staring at their door since it closed. I knew they were a bit drunk, and that meant I might not get any sense out of them, but I also thought it might mean their guard was down and careful questions could reveal some truth.

Before Jermaine could stop me, not that he would but he would counsel against my actions, I took a pace and knocked on their door.

A tirade of expletives erupted from the other side as they began arguing about who was at the door and who was going to answer it. I couldn't really make out what they were saying but the discussion ended when a door slammed somewhere inside the cabin and the door in front of me opened.

'What the fruit do you want?' asked the man, sneering at me without the slightest attempt to hide his disdain. Okay, he didn't say fruit at all, but... well, I'm sure you can substitute his choice of colourful language with one of your own. Let's just say that he said fruit a lot.

I sensed Jermaine tense next to me, but I smiled sweetly when I said, 'Good evening. My name is Patricia Fisher.'

'So fruiting what?' he rudely interrupted.

I pressed on anyway, 'Am I addressing Edgar Brentnall?'

'Who the fruit wants to know?' His willingness to be unpleasant matched his ignorance.

Standing just behind me, Jermaine asked, 'Madam?' I knew what he was asking. He was keen to admonish the man for his rudeness.

Without taking my eyes from Edgar, I said, 'Not yet.' Then answered Edgar's most recent question. 'My name is Patricia Fisher. I am a guest on this ship and was hoping I might be able to ask you a couple of questions.' I remained calm and polite, refraining from pointing out that I had already given him my name. His attitude though was contagious because beneath my placid, serene façade, I fantasised about pushing him down some stairs.

The man's sneer somehow increased in its revulsion as he looked me up and down. Then he slammed the door shut. It didn't shut though, it merely bounced off Jermaine's foot as he stuck it out. Edgar had already turned away, but now spun around to see what had happened and in doing so lost his balance, fetching up against the corner of a couch to keep himself upright.

A door on the far side of the small cabin burst open and Erica exited the bathroom still arranging her undergarments. They were such a delightful couple. 'Who the fruit are you?' she demanded. Then, taking in Edgar as he pushed himself upright, she said, 'What the fruit are you doing, you fruiting banana. Fruit my life, you're fruiting useless.'

He spun on her and raised his hand to strike her. 'What did you say, you utter cumquat?' he snarled. 'I'm going to...'

He didn't get the chance to finish his sentence though as Jermaine stepped neatly around me to grab the man's arm. This elicited a fresh round of expletives as both Erica and Edgar began verbally assaulting Jermaine and each other and, just for good measure, me too.

In the midst of it all, Jermaine let the man's arm go and stepped away. 'Perhaps, madam, we should abandon this line of enquiry for now.'

'Yeah,' yelled Edgar. 'Get the fruit out, you pair of oranges.' He made to shoo Jermaine toward the door, trying to look tough, but he met Jermaine's stony gaze and gave up. I nodded to Jermaine anyway and we left the tiny, smelly cabin behind.

The door slammed behind us once more, shutting us out and sealing off any chance for me to get information from them. Perhaps they would be more reasonable when sober, but I doubted it. Fuelled by their attitude, I was even more determined now to find out how they were involved with the poor man and what they had done to cause his suicide.

Who is Anna? That was the question I most needed an answer to. I couldn't save the man, but I could try to grant his last wish and save the woman, whoever she was.

Anna

It was on the way back up to my suite that I realised Jermaine could look for someone named Anna on the ship's central register. Jermaine replied with, 'The very moment we return, madam.'

He was wrong though, not because we forgot to do so, but because Lieutenant Baker was waiting outside my door. With him was Lieutenant Bhukari, the female security officer who shot Shane Sussmann in my cabin just a few days ago. It was unfortunate that I couldn't look at her without remembering the incident.

Walking from the elevator to my suite took less than a minute but it was long enough for me to glance out the passageway windows to see that the Aurelia was not moving. The great ship had been brought to a dead stop so members of the crew could search the water as they were duty bound to do.

I was still staring out of the windows when Jermaine's single word, 'Madam,' brought my attention back to the present.

'Good evening again, Mrs Fisher,' said Baker with a smile, a similar greeting coming from Deepa Bhukari.

'Have you identified the man?' I asked in response, guessing that it might be the reason for their late evening visit.

Baker shook his head. 'Not yet, Mrs Fisher. Can we talk inside?' His cryptic request was delivered in a quiet voice, making me wonder what he could possibly need to tell me, but Jermaine swiped the entry pad and held the door for everyone to enter before I could ask any questions in the passageway.

With the door closed, I moved into the living area of the suite, placing my handbag on a low side table next to a vase of fresh-cut flowers. 'What can I do for you, Lieutenant Baker?' I asked still crossing the room. I clearly wasn't getting to bed anytime soon and was still reeling a little from the shock of the evening's events.

Jermaine saw my trajectory across the room and asked, 'May I prepare you a night cap, madam?'

He was such a good friend. 'Yes, please. Can I offer one to anyone else?' I asked the two uniformed crew as I slumped, less than elegantly, into a high-backed armchair arranged with other chairs and a couch around a coffee table.

If Baker and Bhukari were tempted, they resisted well, and I probably shouldn't have offered as they were both clearly on duty. Instead, having declined the drink, Baker said, 'I wanted to ask if you remembered anything else about the man you saw, Mrs Fisher.'

Bhukari added, 'Can you remember what he said?'

I found it odd they were asking questions I had already answered. 'Commander Shriver took a description from me already. Would you like me to repeat it?'

'Yes, please,' replied Baker, taking out a notebook to write in.

I went through my description again, picturing the man as best I could to get it right. Somewhere on board he had a wife who would soon be asking where her husband was. That was when I realised I hadn't told them about Anna earlier. 'He asked me to save Anna.' They both looked up from the notepad which they were suspiciously not writing in. To answer the question they were about to ask, I said, 'I don't know who that is. They were his last words though. He asked me to save Anna and then he jumped. Given that he was wearing a wedding ring, I think we should assume that Anna is his wife and she is somewhere on board this boat.'

Behind me, Jermaine moved to the computer, pressing the button to fire it up. He did so as he brought my gin and tonic, the cold, harsh liquid welcome as I thanked him and took a deep gulp.

Baker and Bhukari looked back down at the notepad but it was clear they were both reading whatever was written there and not making fresh notes. Frustrated and tired, I tapped my hand loudly on the arm of my chair to get their attention. In the space of the last few weeks, I had learned that leadership was generally welcomed provided it was strong, determined, and respectful. I was in charge here, so I steered the conversation the direction I wanted it to go. Right now, I wanted to know what was going on.

'What are you reading?' I asked their surprised faces. When I saw Baker's cheeks redden slightly, I pinned him in place with a laser stare. 'You haven't written down anything I have said, so what is it?'

'Um...' he started. 'Um, we were tasked with...'

'With what?' I snapped, jolting him into getting on with it.

It was Deepa Bhukari who answered though. With a sigh, she said, 'Commander Shriver wanted us to check your description now to the description you gave earlier.'

'What on earth for?' I started to ask but then realisation dawned. 'Because she wasn't convinced I saw anyone jump. Was she?' I was nodding as I spoke, able to see the truth of it. 'Mrs Fisher, always in the thick of it hasn't had any attention for a few days so invents a suicide that no one can prove or disprove.'

No one said anything. Annoyed, I drank another glug of my gin and waited for the two lieutenants to say something. Baker looked embarrassed and I sensed that he had probably come here unwillingly on the orders of Commander Shriver. Just then, the familiar rumble that had been strangely absent returned: the propellers were turning again as the ship restarted its journey.

I stood and brushed imaginary creases from the front of my dress, looking up when I was ready to fix the two crew with a disappointed look. 'Please assure Commander Shriver that she is missing a passenger. I will do my best to find out who the man was and will let her know when I do.' I dismissed them then, picking up my glass and turning away as I went to the computer. 'If, in the meantime, a lady called Anna reports a missing person, you will know where to direct Commander Shriver's apology.'

Jermaine pulled out the chair at the computer desk for me to sit down and slid it in beneath me. When neither lieutenant moved, I said, 'You can let yourselves out.' I was being rude, and I knew that it wasn't their intention to upset me. Nevertheless, a man was dead, taking his own life rather than face whatever it was the couple in 2124 had in store for him. No one was doing anything about it, but he left behind a widow who at this time possibly didn't even know her husband wasn't coming back. It irked me greatly.

Jermaine helped me navigate to the ship's central register of passengers; something I wasn't supposed to have access to, and there we began our search. I was fuelled up and had a fire in my belly. If Commander Shriver believed I invented the suicide, I would present her with the answers in the morning.

The Gym

It was almost two in the morning when I climbed into bed, and then I only called it quits because Jermaine insisted on staying up with me. I expected to sleep fitfully despite the two industrial-strength gins in my bloodstream, but I rested dreamlessly, no haunting images of the man's face causing me to wake until my natural rhythm pulled me to consciousness just before six.

There were twelve ladies called Anna on board the Aurelia, three of whom were crew. The crew members were easy to dismiss as they were unmarried which left nine, of which four could be discounted due to their age. In fact, three of the four were travelling with another lady and had a listed age of over seventy. That left five and I was able to eliminate one more by determining that her partner, listed as Susan, probably wasn't the man I saw last night.

Armed with four names and four cabin numbers, I would take a walk when the hour was a little more decent and see if I could find the poor widow. I wasn't sure what I was going to do when I did though. Surely, by now, the woman must have reported her missing husband and the crew must have identified the man that jumped, connecting a picture she must have on her phone or in her purse to the description I gave them. If not, would it fall to me to deliver the news? It shouldn't, but I couldn't imagine how I would avoid it if I found her and she didn't already know. It was a stress-inducing thought.

I slid from my bed, dressed and was about to leave my bedroom when I remembered we were due to dock in Tokyo in the early hours of the morning. I pulled open my curtains, instantly dazzled by the bright sunlight shining in from outside. It was early morning, but my view was filled with a bustling dockside, filled with life as busy workers went back and forth. We were still coming alongside, undoubtedly delayed by a couple of hours because the ship stopped to search for the man.

The Tokyo skyline stretched into the distance, drawing my eye beyond the derricks on the dockside to take in huge glass and chrome buildings that must provide an impressive backdrop at night. I would get to explore it soon enough, but only once I had borne out my duty to the man and found Anna. It was too early to do that now, but my nervous energy was already building, so I changed my clothes for gym gear, grabbed a bottle of water from the refrigerator and let myself out. Barbie would be in the gym already. Despite the fact that she would have the next two days off and could relax, I was certain I would find her in the gym either getting in a workout or perhaps working on one of her project customers. Barbie gave her time freely to those who wanted to improve their health or get stronger, regularly taking on people who had been avoiding the gym for most of their lives. I had been one such project and felt vastly different now that I was exercising and testing myself on a regular basis. Barbie assured me I would improve my fitness and drop far more unnecessary bodyfat if I cut out the gin, but who has time for that?

Barbie was a sweet girl from California and a gym instructor with qualifications to suit. We bonded in my early days on board and she considered Jermaine to be her best friend on the ship's crew so often came to my suite just to see him. She had offered to come ashore with me today which I think was because she knew I was travelling alone. My day was already arranged when she asked though; I was heading into Tokyo with two retired cops from Hawaii. I met them two days ago when they deliberately sought me out. Apparently, the missing sapphire case came to their attention because they were tracking news about the Aurelia; they were due to board her after all. So, when they saw the story, they read it with interest. I got on great with them, the two men were like a comedy double act, constantly making me laugh while poking fun at each other.

Sadly, they met a few years ago because their wives were both terminally ill with cancer. They didn't know each other at the time even though they were both cops for over forty years and very similar in age. They knew lots of the same people though and laughed that they had probably stood next to each other on duty at some point and never realised.

When we last spoke on the subject, Barbie had been undecided about what to do with her day. This was her second trip to Tokyo, and she didn't seem overtly enthralled with the place, but I hoped she would join us to make it an even foursome.

As expected, when I pushed open the door to the gym, there she was. 'Hi, Barbie,' I called out and waved as I made my way to the cardio and weights area.

She was barefoot on a mat in front of a mirror with a barbell above her head. I got a breathless, 'Hey, Patty,' in reply as she dropped her bottom to the floor again, performing another overhead squat; an exercise I found particularly hard. I waited patiently while she finished her set and put the barbell back on the floor. I felt exhausted just watching her.

She took on some water, then turned away from the mirror to greet me properly. Her face though, bore a trace of concern. 'Jermaine told me what happened last night. Are you okay?' she asked.

The little rat had blabbed. With good intention of course, but still. 'I'm fine. How much do you know?'

'Only that Jermaine is concerned you are on a quest to find a woman that might need saving from something or someone and that you already had a run in with two unsavoury characters.' Barbie was eyeing me suspiciously as she asked, 'Are you going to get into trouble again?'

I shrugged and gave her a wry smile. 'Probably. Commander Shriver deemed my report of events to be… questionable. Somewhere on this ship is a wife that is now a widow and I am not sure anyone is doing anything about it.'

'That doesn't mean you have to, Patty.' Barbie was just being concerned but she hadn't looked into the man's eyes when he begged for help.

'Someone has to,' I replied, my tone solemn and committed. 'He asked me to save Anna. Whatever his reason was for committing suicide, he thought the danger to him would extend to Anna. For all I know, the poor woman is in mortal danger.'

My reasoning didn't swing Barbie's vote though. Instead she argued, 'All the more reason for you to stay out of it, Patty. What if she is in danger? It's the ship's security team that need to get involved.'

I nodded at her statement rather than argue with it. She was right, but she was also wrong. 'If Commander Shriver isn't yet dedicating any manpower to finding the woman, it might be too late by the time she does. All I intend to do is identify who Anna is and in turn identify who the man lost at sea was. Once that is done, I will stay out of the way and… go eat sushi or something. I don't want drama and trouble. I just need to reassure myself that Anna will be saved.'

'Saved from what?' asked Barbie.

I shrugged again. It was becoming a habit. 'No idea. Hopefully that will all become clear when I find her. It's still too early to be knocking on doors, but in an hour, people will be up and getting ready to go ashore. By then, it won't matter if I get a couple of wrong doors first.'

Satisfied somewhat by my answers, Barbie looked about at the weights and equipment around us, then back at me. 'Um, you're wearing sports gear, were you planning a workout before the sleuthing?'

That was my intention, so even though I didn't really feel like it, I knew that some physical activity would distract me from the questions bouncing around in my head. I soon regretted telling Barbie my reason though as five minutes later I couldn't breathe and there seemed to be too little oxygen getting to my brain. I will admit that it worked though; I was too busy trying to stay alive to worry about Anna.

After forty minutes of CrossFit style movements and cardio, I collapsed on the mat begging for mercy.

'You're so funny, Patty,' Barbie laughed. If only I was joking. 'What's next then?' she asked, barely out of breath even though she had mirrored my movements to act as a pacemaker.

I held up a hand to beg for a moment's grace. Then, when I felt I could complete a sentence without having to gasp for breath, I said, 'I'm going to get a shower and change, then knock on a couple of doors.'

She pursed her lips, clearly not entirely happy that I was involving myself in what I described as a potentially dangerous situation. 'Assuming you find her, what then?' she asked.

It was a good question, but one I had already considered. 'I ask her to let me into her cabin and call security from there. It is not my place to tell the woman her husband is dead. It seems ridiculous that she might not know or might not have reported his absence. Perhaps, if she hasn't, it is to do with whatever he was mixed up in. Anyway, I will hand over to

Commander Shriver and move on with my life.' Barbie raised a single eyebrow. 'Honest,' I protested. 'I have no intention of getting mixed up in anything.'

'Okay, Patty,' she replied, but she didn't sound like she believed me.

As I turned to go, I remembered the plan to go ashore together and turned around again so I could talk to her. 'Barbie, did you decide what you wanted to do today? Akamu and Rick would love to have you along. Neither of them has ever been to Japan either so maybe you could be Tour Guide Barbie for the day?'

The different Barbie names had started in Hawaii when Jermaine bought a Hawaiian Barbie doll as a fun gift for her when he saw it in a shop window. It was a knock off version but after that, if she got drinks, she was Bartender Barbie, if she put on a swimsuit, she was Swimsuit Barbie. The names just rolled off the tongue and she took it in good humour.

'Tour Guide Barbie, huh?' she smiled. 'Look... I think I'm going to pass. I didn't really enjoy Tokyo last time.' She saw me looking at her for a reason why, so added, 'I got a bit too much attention from the Japanese men. Something to do with being tall and blonde, I think. It was creepy. So, if it's all the same to you. I think I will stay on board. We're going to India next. I'll get off there. That place is beautiful.'

I said, 'Okay.' She was clearly uncomfortable about going ashore so I wasn't going to push it. A glance at the clock told me I needed to get a move on, so I bade her a good day and went back to the suite to prepare for the day ahead.

At my request, Jermaine had breakfast waiting for me when I emerged, clean and fresh, from my bedroom. The clock was ticking though, and I did not want to run the risk that I would miss my potential Annas as people would soon be heading for the exit. Jermaine raised one eyebrow in surprise but didn't comment when I wolfed down the scrambled eggs and smoked salmon. I swigged the hot fresh coffee, which was only just cool enough to drink, then grabbed my bag, thanked him for the wonderful spread and ran to the door.

I probably didn't need to rush the way I was, but I couldn't tell how long it would take me to find the four different cabins or whether the Anna I wanted would be in the first one or the last one. I was also conscious that the time I then spent with the right Anna might stretch to more than an hour, depending on how quickly the security team reacted, and I was due to meet Rick and Akamu at nine thirty; it was already coming up on eight.

The first cabin I tried was on the eighteenth deck on the port side. If I had the ship worked out correctly, it should have a sea view which meant it would be on my right as I walked down the passageway. I found it easily enough, but as I raised my hand to knock on the door, butterflies started flitting about in my stomach. What was I going to find on the other side of the door? It felt like playing Russian roulette because sooner or later I was going to find the tear-soaked widow.

Forcing myself to take a calming breath, I rapped three hard knocks, then waited for the door to open.

Nothing happened.

Feeling a little anti-climactic, given how much I had built up to the moment, I let my shoulders slump, releasing the tension keeping me rigidly upright. My foot twitched to walk away but I figured I might as well knock again or maybe even call out in case the lady inside was afraid – if she was in danger, maybe she didn't want to answer the door.

As I raised my hand to knock again though, the door snapped open and a cheerful and excited couple in their late thirties attempted to leave, all but bumping into me as they came through the door. My presence startled them just as they startled me.

'Gosh. Hi, can we help you?' asked the man, pausing because I blocked his path. He was a tall, lean Caucasian man with a mid-western accent. His wide-hipped wife didn't speak but I could already see that if the lady's name was Anna, she was not the one I was looking for.

Thinking on the spot, I said, 'Sorry, wrong cabin. I was looking for my friends.' Then, because we were all staring at each other and not speaking, I said brightly, 'Have fun today. It looks like the weather will be kind to us.' They said similar things in response, and I stepped back to let them go on their way.

Strike one.

The next cabin on my list was on the same deck but around toward the starboard side and further back toward the stern. Once again, I found it easily enough and once again the butterflies began to rise as I raised my hand to knock on the door – the odds that this was the right cabin had increased.

My hopes were soon dashed though when an African gentleman opened the door. His wife, also African, was visible in the cabin behind him, packing a backpack for the day ahead. I used the same apology and excuse of having the wrong cabin, this time pretending I was on the wrong floor. He nodded politely and closed the door as I moved away.

I wasn't doing very well, but the odds that it was the next room were now fifty-fifty.

'Hey, Patricia,' called a familiar voice from behind me. 'Are you looking for us?' I turned around to find Rick and Akamu in the passageway behind me. They were coming out of a cabin, but I hadn't known their cabin was on this deck; asking a gentleman, or worse yet, gentlemen, where they are sleeping, isn't the done thing.

'Hi, guys,' I replied with a wave.

Akamu waved back as he shut the door and made sure it was locked. It was Rick that called to get my attention and now the pair of them were shuffling my way. They were both well into their seventies and getting a little decrepit. Not to the point that they needed Zimmer frames or walking sticks, but they weren't going running anytime soon. They were dressed very similarly with polo shirts tucked into knee length shorts and white tube socks pulled halfway up their shins. It was the first time I had seen Akamu without an Hawaiian shirt on as if it was a matter of national pride that he wore one.

'Were you looking for us?' Rick repeated, slowing his shuffle as he neared me.

I smiled and air-kissed both men as I greeted them, then said, 'I wasn't actually. I was trying to find someone.'

'Find someone?' Rick echoed, looking curious.

'Ooh,' said Akamu, gripping his friend's shoulder in excitement. 'Are you solving a mystery?' he asked, his voice an octave higher.

29

Rick turned to face him. 'What just happened to your voice?'

Akamu frowned. 'What?'

'Your voice. It just went from Hawaiian man to Doris Day. Are you feeling alright? Should I expect a musical number?' Rick was finding something to poke fun at and wasting no time in doing so.

Akamu wasn't going to let the salvo go unanswered though. 'Why? Are you hoping for a tune to dance to? Maybe pop a hip as you bust some moves, you decrepit old fool.' Before Rick could open a new line of banter, Akamu repeated his question, this time in his usual baritone, 'Are you solving a mystery, Patricia?'

'No, not really,' I replied, then, worried that I was sort of lying, I explained about the man that jumped.

Both men grimaced when I described watching him disappear beneath the waves. 'Drowning,' said Akamu with a shudder. 'That's got to be a terrible way to go.'

'With a weight around him, he would sink so quickly his lungs would implode from the pressure before he had a chance to drown,' replied Rick, sounding knowledgeable.

'No, he wouldn't,' argued Akamu. 'Where do you get your daft ideas?'

As the pair took to light-hearted squabbling again, I said, 'I have to keep going,' and backed away a couple of paces which brought their attention back to me.

'You didn't tell us who you were looking for yet?' complained Rick, shuffling after me. So, I explained as I led them to the nearest elevator bank; the next cabin on my list was three decks down. By the time we got there, they knew everything that I knew and were reminiscing about their early careers as beat cops and having to deliver notice of death to unknowing spouses and parents. It sounded like a terrible thing to have to do, but that, essentially, was what I had planned.

Finding the third cabin on my list, I once again knocked on the door, the familiar fluttering feeling in my middle worse this time as I felt certain this would be the one. A small oriental boy opened the door. He looked Japanese to me and my heart sank as I realised I had failed to consider that the man might also have children. Would the child speak English though? Would Anna? I was expecting her to be Japanese just because her husband was, but his ability to speak English didn't mean she would.

I was still thinking all this when Rick spoke. 'Is your mommy in?' he asked the boy.

The boy let go of the door and turned away looking bored. He shouted, 'Mom, there's some old people at the door.' He wasn't Japanese at all. Or, at least, I was going to be surprised if he held a Japanese passport; he was from Hawaii.

As the boy disappeared, clearly unconcerned about exposing the cabin to strangers, a woman moved into view. She was at a dressing table across the room using a pair of hair straighteners on her shiny jet-black hair. Seeing us, she put them down carefully and crossed the room to see what we wanted.

Rick gave her a friendly wave as she approached, but we all kept our faces sombre. 'Can I help you?' she asked.

'Anna?' I asked, searching her face for a reaction.

Her reply came with a curious expression. 'Yes.' How was it that the stranger at her door knew her name?

31

'My name is Patricia Fisher,' I introduced myself but moved quickly onto the dreadful task. 'I believe I need to speak to you about your husband.' The woman's eyes widened. 'Can I ask when you last saw him?'

'Oh, my God! Has something happened to him?' she blurted her question, then clamped her hand over her mouth and glanced into the cabin behind her to see if her little boy was listening. He wasn't but the woman was already panicking. 'Tell me,' she demanded quietly. Then, before I could speak again, her brow knitted in confusion and she said, 'Hold on. Who did you say you were again? Why isn't it someone from the Navy?'

'The Navy?' I repeated, now confused myself.

'Yes,' the woman said, now looking less worried and more suspicious. 'If my husband has been hurt or worse in service, it should be someone from the US Navy that tells me. You don't even sound American.'

I shook my head to clear it, suddenly worried that this wasn't the right Anna after all. Akamu got a question in first though. 'Your husband is currently serving on a ship somewhere?'

She turned her eyes toward him as she answered, 'Yes. He's been in the Persian Gulf on the USS Dow Jones for the last six weeks. I'm on my way to visit my parents in Yokohama. Has something happened to him?'

'We are terribly sorry to have troubled you, Anna,' replied Akamu. He was already backing away. 'We have the wrong cabin. Please forgive us.' Anna looked like she wanted to say something, but as we all backed away looking embarrassed, she simply closed the door on our faces.

'Goodness, that was awful,' I commented, thankful that I hadn't just told the women her husband was dead.

'Did you say there was one cabin left to try?' asked Rick. I nodded that there was, but my determination to find Anna had been replaced with a desperate hope that I wouldn't. 'Where is it?'

The answer to Rick's question was all the way down on the ninth deck. I gave them the cabin number but didn't voice my trepidation about going there. I had struck out three times now. Didn't that mean my turn was over? Sadly, I knew that no one else was going to do the task for me and not knowing would claw at me all day.

Though we could use elevators to get down to the twelfth deck, the cabin was right at the stern of the ship and we were not walking fast. What might have taken me fifteen minutes, took at least ten more than that, Rick and Akamu shuffling along chatting amiably about what they wanted to do with their day. The pair of them often reminisced about their wives and how much they would have enjoyed the trip.

Eventually, we found the door to the cabin that contained the last Anna on the ship. I felt dreadful as I raised my hand to knock on the door, but I did it anyway, rapping hard three times then standing back so I wasn't crowding the door. Noise on the other side preceded the door opening and my heart started thumping in my chest as I prepared myself for the terrible few minutes to follow.

Then the door swung open and a man said, 'Hello. Oh, I was expecting someone else.' He peered around the door frame to look along the passageway, saw no one and brought his attention back to me. 'Um, can I help you?'

I let my shoulders slump in defeat. 'No. Sorry, it would seem I have made a mistake.' I was staring at the deck wondering how I had managed to make such a mess of it. Had I misheard what the man had said? It sounded like Anna at the time, but... I felt a light tug on my elbow. Rick was trying to pull me away from the man's door.

'Who is it, darling?' called a woman's voice from inside the cabin.

'Um,' the man wasn't sure how to reply to that question.

'Sorry. We'll be going now,' said Rick, taking a better grip on my elbow so he could turn me around. When I glanced back, the cabin door was shut again. Sensing my embarrassment, Rick and Akamu started chatting again. 'Akamu, did you know they have a café here where there are owls on the table for you to pet?' Rick asked.

'I did not know that,' replied Akamu. It was all very forced and fake, but they were being polite and sensitive to my feelings.

I interrupted before they started discussing the make-believe café. 'Guys, I'm sorry. That was a complete waste of your time. I'm... I'm not sure now whether I heard the man correctly. I swear he asked me to save Anna. Now I don't know what to think.'

'We came along voluntarily,' Akamu reminded me. 'Besides, Rick and I have both followed plenty of dead end leads in our time. Haven't we, Rick?'

'Sure have,' Rick agreed. 'So, what do we do next?' he asked.

I pursed my lips in thought. 'I think we should go ashore and enjoy our day.' I couldn't think what else there was that we could do. I had no leads, I still didn't know the man's name, and it seemed very possible that I had misheard his last request. I nodded my head. 'Yes, I think we should just forget about it and explore Tokyo.'

As we arrived at the elevator, Akamu asked, 'Are we still doing the coach trip to Mount Fuji tomorrow?'

Rick looked at me expectantly. 'I can't think why not.' I smiled at them both, but I couldn't shake the feeling that I had a duty to perform to the dead man. If I didn't work out who Anna was and make sure she was safe, then who would? I needed to work out who he was so I could work out if there was someone called Anna in his life. Maybe he said Anne not Anna. I hadn't searched for anyone called Anne.

The elevator pinged and the doors swished open. The car was half full and picked up more people on the next deck. Passengers were heading to the exit, all keen to leave the ship after a lengthy passage.

I was deep in thought still, trying to tell myself to leave it alone but also still trying to work the problem in my head. I was so lost inside my own head that I nearly wet myself when Rick touched my shoulder. 'Is your friend still joining us today?' he asked.

'What friend?' I asked, forgetting that they met Barbie a couple of days ago.

'The blonde one. You know...' He was struggling for a name. 'The one with the unbelievable boobs,' he concluded, hoping that was enough description to go on.

It was, of course. 'You mean, Barbie,' I replied. 'No, I don't think so.' The elevator stopped at the eighth deck, the last stop before we all needed to get off, but as the doors opened to let more people on, my heart stopped beating.

The couple from cabin 2124 were getting on.

Quickly, I turned around to face the back of the car. It brought me face to face with an oriental man and into his personal space. He was short which placed his eyes at the same height as my chest. He was trying to find somewhere else to look and had to settle on staring at the ceiling while his wife glared at me.

'What are you doing?' asked Rick. He was standing to my right, which, having turned around, was now my left.

I was the only one in the elevator facing the wrong way, but I hissed quietly, 'That's them.'

Akamu leaned in so he could hear too. 'Them who?' he asked.

'The couple from cabin 2124,' I hissed as quietly as I could. I risked a quick glance over my shoulder, wanting to see if the couple recognised me when the doors opened and were now staring in my direction. They were closed again so I was trapped but they were facing the doors and paying no attention to anything in the elevator car.

Akamu and Rick both stared at the couple. They were right in front of the doors, but they were the tallest and broadest people in the small space so could be seen even though there were twenty people between us. As if sensing our scrutiny, Edgar, then Erica both glanced backward. My friends pretended to be looking at nothing but if the couple were suspicious, they didn't have time to react because the elevator pinged, and everyone started moving forward to get off. At the front of the car, they were swept out and away.

I breathed a sigh of relief and sagged against the wall while Rick held the door for me. As I gathered myself and left the car, he said, 'I see what you mean about them. They look like hardened criminals, not cruise ship passengers.'

'We should follow them,' said Akamu, sounding excited.

'Yeah,' agreed Rick. 'Let's see what they are up to. Maybe they can lead us to Anna.'

Suddenly, I was back in the hunt. 'What about your plans for the day?' I asked.

Rick punched his right fist into his left hand. 'Hah! This sounds way more exciting than some café with owls in it.'

'I thought you made that up?' questioned Akamu.

'No. It's a real thing,' Rick insisted.

Akamu cocked an eyebrow. 'You're full of it.'

'Am not. I'll prove it, you silly, fat old islander.'

Sensing that they were descending into one of their deliberately drawn out squabbling sessions, I interrupted. 'They are leaving,' I said as I pointed. We were walking, slowly because I was with two geriatric gentlemen, but ahead of us was a queue of passengers squeezing through the exit barriers to leave the ship and the tall couple from cabin 2124 were forcing their way through rather than wait politely at the back. If we didn't hurry, we were going to lose them.

'Patty!' I heard Barbie's voice ring out from somewhere behind me but couldn't see her until she jumped to get her head above the crowd.

'Goodness,' said Rick. 'I could watch her jump about all day.' He might be geriatric but there didn't seem to be much wrong with his eyes - or his libido. Barbie was jumping about to attract our attention and her chest was doing interesting things inside her top.

I waved to show that I had seen her but then had to watch Edgar and Erica shove their way to the front of the queue while we waited for Barbie to catch up.

'I changed my mind,' she said with a smile and a quick wave to Rick and Akamu. 'Staying on board for two days just seems senseless and I am sure I will draw far less attention with my two lovely chaperones.' With that she looped her left arm through Rick's right and then her right arm through Akamu's left and began leading them to a passageway on the left.

'Where are you going?' I called after her. 'We need to go this way.'

'Crew exit,' she called out, hurrying away as fast as the two old men could go. 'No queue,' her voice drifted back as she vanished.

I jogged after her, and sure enough, just around a corner, was an exit I had never noticed before. To be fair, I usually enter and exit through the royal suite entrance more than two hundred yards further toward the prow of the ship. There was no queue at the crew exit though, so having scanned ourselves out, we arrived on the quayside before the Brentnalls.

'So, what's first on the agenda?' asked Barbie excitedly. 'Did you have breakfast already? I know a wonderful place not far from here that the captain showed me on my first visit. Did you know Patty is good friends with the captain?' she asked Rick and Akamu with a cheeky wink at me. Her brain was bouncing from thought to thought as it often did when she got excited. We hadn't told her about the alternate plan for our day yet, so as my cheeks warmed and I hid my face behind a large pair of designer sunglasses, I started to explain about the Brentnalls.

38

She caught on quickly, sensing the urgent nature of our next move if we were to follow them. So, when Rick pointed them out a minute later as the ugly couple came into the sunshine outside the ship, Barbie reacted by flagging down a cab.

I say that she flagged it down, but the line of cabs just across from us were in an orderly queue and being controlled by a pair of stewards from the ship. The line was constantly creeping forward with new cars joining the back all the time. Barbie skipped quickly across the tarmac to the very last car and leaned down to speak with the driver. She didn't crouch though, she bent at the waist which ensured the driver got a very good look at the goods on offer inside her summer dress. Convincing the man to cut the queue took about four seconds and she had the back door open for the three older people before he could realise what was happening.

Whatever it was he had hoped for, he soon realised he'd been conned when his eyes swung from the bulbous delights in front of his face, to the old codgers shuffling in his direction. His grin vanished instantly.

We all piled into the back seats as Barbie addressed the driver, 'This is ever so kind of you.' She checked my two older friends were settled in their seats, then plopped into the front next to the driver. 'Hideki, this is Patty, Rick and Akamu. Everyone, this is Hideki.'

He got a polite konnichi wa from each of us in the backseat, but he replied with, 'Yeah, whatever,' his English surprisingly good but accompanied by a sigh as he put the car into gear and asked, 'Where to?'

'Actually,' I started to say, 'Can you see the tall couple just about to get into a cab at the front of the queue?'

He lifted himself up a bit in his seat to get a better view. 'The ones that look like graverobbers?' he clarified.

His description was bang on accurate. 'Yes, that's them, well...'

'Follow that cab!' urged Rick, gushing with excitement.

The cab driver grimaced at the clichéd instruction, but he checked his mirror and pulled into traffic as the cab with the Brentnalls inside pulled away. 'Any idea where they are going?' he asked.

His question wasn't really aimed at anyone in particular but he glanced at Barbie for an answer and she in turn looked behind her to see if we knew.

I shrugged. 'Not the faintest idea. They are up to something and we want to know what it is.' My reply didn't placate the man though.

Instead, he looked worried. 'Is this going to cause trouble? I don't want any trouble. Not with people that look like that.'

The driver clearly meant the Brentnalls, but Akamu said, 'Trouble? Look at us. We have a combined age of about three-hundred and fifty years between us. Trouble is not on the agenda.' He delivered the line with a chuckle, but I wondered if it would hold true.

The road from the dock was slow moving at first, then picked up as we joined a dual carriageway and then a motorway. We were heading in a direct line for the centre of Tokyo by the looks of things but were still many miles from the huge glass towers that dominated the skyline.

Following the Brentnall's cab was easy enough. Their driver had no reason to check for a tail and there were yellow cabs everywhere so even if he had been looking, he wouldn't have seen anything suspicious. Also, their cab had an advert for a popular global haemorrhoid cream on its tail which made it easy to spot among the others. As we drifted along in the other cab's wake, the driver started jabbering away at us. 'You are American, yes?' he asked.

I knew he was picking up on the other accents in the group, but with a touch of indignation I said, 'British.'

'Oh? You are not American?' the question was aimed at Barbie.

She smiled pleasantly. 'I'm from Los Angeles.'

'And we're from Hawaii!' yelled Akamu, never one to shy away from announcing his heritage.

'Oh, hai! Hawaii 5-O!' replied the driver, happy that he could make a cultural reference. Then he started singing the tune song to the old show. 'Pa-pa pa-pa, pah, pah, pa-pa-pa-pa, pah!' Then Akamu joined in, happy as a pig in muck and he slapped Rick in his ribs to get him to sing as well. Laughing from the front seat, Barbie added her voice and suddenly Akamu was playing a set of imaginary drums.

I began to feel very self-conscious that I wasn't playing along, but as my friends and the cab driver built to the big crescendo, I shoved my arm through the gap between the front seats. 'They're pulling off!' I interrupted, having to shout to make myself heard.

The singing stopped abruptly as the driver came back to the here and now, saw a limited window of chance and threw the steering wheel to the left to get us through a gap and down the same off-ramp. We all braced ourselves as he narrowly missed the nose of a car and zipped through the gap to a blast of horn.

For the previous fifteen minutes of journey, the huge glass towers of the city had slowly loomed ever bigger in the windscreen as the motorway took us into the city proper. Now, we were descending from a raised and

41

modern-looking four-lane motorway into a dodgy-looking, litter-strewn suburb.

'You want me to keep following them?' the driver asked. 'This isn't the nicest district they are going into. Maybe I should take you nice folks to a museum instead. They have an exhibition of 17th century Japanese artists in the new wing of the Tokyo Metropolitan. It just opened a few days ago.'

Looking at the tattoo parlours between derelict buildings and the increasing level of graffiti we faced, I wondered if the cab driver might not be the voice of reason, but we had come this far and I was sure there was no real danger despite my paranoia.

Barbie swung her head around to check my opinion, but we continued on. 'We could stay in the car once we see where they are going,' she suggested.

'Yeah,' agreed Rick. 'Although, it's not all that comfortable back here and I think Akamu farted.'

'That's your breath,' his friend fired back.

There were fewer taxis here, so we were more visible, or so I told myself. The Brentnalls ought to have no reason to be checking behind for a tail, but if they were the criminals they looked to be, they might have it built in as a reflex.

'What on earth are Aurelia guests doing somewhere so dodgy?' asked Barbie. The question was aimed at no one in particular and no one answered. She was right though. There was no way they were engaged in normal tourist activities coming to this part of the city. Then the lights ahead of us changed and our target slipped through while we got stuck. Rick swore and we all tried to see where their cab went as it crossed the junction and vanished up a side street. The light didn't hold us up for more than a minute, so when it changed, I thought we might be able to catch up to them.

'They must be close to their destination,' Rick explained. 'We are in the back streets so they can't be going through here to get to somewhere else.'

'Let's hope so,' I murmured in response.

We crossed the junction, easing down a narrow street between rundown businesses that might have been illegal gambling dens or brothels or maybe even something worse than that, and I wondered again if this was such a good idea.

Hideki saw my expression in his rear-view mirror, my eyes flicking up to catch his. 'Don't worry, missus. If the storefronts look bad there's probably not much to worry about. It's the nice-looking ones you have to be wary of.' Sage words. I hoped I wouldn't find out how accurate they were.

He reached the side street the Brentnall's cab had taken but it was nowhere in sight. In fact, the street was devoid of cars, but it was nothing more than a short passage between two buildings; an alleyway more than it was a street. Hideki sped up to get through it, emerging at the other end where we all scanned around for the cab.

'There,' squealed Barbie. 'That's it, isn't it?'

I could see the haemorrhoid cream advert on the cab's back end. 'It sure is! Can you catch up to it?'

Akamu's brow ruffled in a frown. 'How can you be certain that's the one?'

'It's… I just can.' I couldn't think of a good way to introduce bum cream into a polite conversation, so I deftly avoided doing so.

'It's got an advertisement for butthole cream on the back of it. You should recognise it; it's the same one you use,' Rick snapped at his friend, getting a quick salvo in. Akamu didn't respond though because we caught up to the cab in traffic and it was clear to all of us that the occupants were no longer in it.

Rick swore again, then swivelled in his seat to look out the back window. 'It was only out of our sight for a minute and now it's empty. They must have got out in that side street. Anywhere else and we would have seen them.'

'He must be right, Patty,' agreed Barbie. 'Shall we double back and look for them?'

The driver was already turning the cab around to double back, the move a difficult one in moving traffic. It gave me a few seconds to think. 'I don't know. I don't want to expose anyone to a dangerous situation.'

'Are you kidding me?' asked Akamu. 'Rick thinks he's Steve McGarrett. We get in any trouble and he'll just pop a cap in someone's ass.'

Rick laughed. 'Yeah, and then I'll tell you to book 'em, Danno.'

'I'm confused,' said Barbie. She was hanging between the front seat to look at those of us in the back and crinkling her forehead. 'Who is Danno?' Barbie was about twenty-five years too young to remember the original Hawaii 5-O series even though she knew the music for it. There was no time for me to explain though as Hideki was back at the side street and about to turn down it once more.

'This will do right here,' Rick told the driver, pulling his wallet from a back pocket to pay the fare. He saw me about to argue and cut me off, 'You can get lunch.' Before I could argue about who was paying or whether we should even be getting out, the other three were opening doors and leaving me behind.

I shuffled across the seat to catch up. 'Good luck, lady,' said Hideki as I slid out of the back door. Then, just as I closed it, I heard him say to himself, 'You're going to need it.'

We were alone on the sidewalk in a back alley. There wasn't another person in sight but there were noises coming from the street ahead of us and the two older men were already shuffling towards it. 'I can smell food,' Rick called over his shoulder. 'There has to be something to eat around here somewhere, I'm starving.'

He was right about the smell; spicy aromas were drifting on the air and as we neared the corner, I could make out the sound of pans being rattled. Since I had no idea where the Brentnalls had gone, this direction was as good as any other. Maybe they had been to Tokyo before and knew a great place for breakfast.

The street we turned into was a marketplace, filled with stalls selling all manner of goods and there were several places with open flames cooking food. Unfamiliar with the dishes, my knowledge of Japanese cuisine started and ended with sushi but that was not what was on offer. Rick made a beeline for an elderly woman tossing some kind of meat on a hot plate. The hotplate itself was little more than a piece of sheet steel with a flame beneath it but the food on top smelled and looked good.

I scanned around for the Brentnalls, confident they would be easy to spot because of their size. Up and down the street, there were stalls with people buying and selling but no sign of the English couple.

'Do you see them?' asked Barbie.

I shook my head. 'Not yet.'

'This is good,' Rick mumbled around a mouthful of food.

Barbie turned to look at him. There was grease running over his fingers. 'What is it?' she asked.

'No idea,' he mumbled back. 'It's good though.' He was stuffing his face, but I figured he could walk and eat so I set off further along the line of businesses.

As we moved along the line of stalls, a greasy-looking Japanese man in a cheap suit appeared. He didn't fit in with the other people around him and I noticed that the stall holders kept out of his way. He was watching us as we moved along the street, tracking our movements and talking to someone unseen.

When I next glanced across, he had vanished, but appeared just a few seconds later in front of us, effectively blocking our path in the narrow street. 'Hey, pretty ladies, you want to win some money? Lots of good games today. I bet you win big time. Right this way,' he leered at us with a broken-toothed smile. He was short, which is to say that he was about my height and his black hair was slicked back from his forehead to hang down his back. His right arm was out to guide us away from the street to wherever it was he wanted us to go.

'No, thank you,' replied Rick.

The smiling Japanese man shot Rick an angry glare, then looked back at Barbie and smiled again. 'This way, please. Best games in Tokyo. Free drinks while you play.'

'No, thank you,' echoed Barbie, getting her answer in before I could.

'Aw, come on, pretty lady. Don't break my heart,' the little man drawled. I could see where he was pointing, and though I didn't know what an illegal gambling den looked like, if I had to draw one, it would look like the building he wanted to take us in. A heavily tattooed and very large pair of men were standing at the door. As I looked, they both gave me a smile, though they looked like they would just as happily bury me at the nearest landfill site. Hideki was right; we should have stayed in the cab.

'One game, one drink,' the little man begged. 'I bet you win first time.'

Rick took a pace forward. 'It's a scam,' he said as he tried to push by the little man. A scrawny arm shot out to grab Rick's elbow, pinning him in place as he cut his eyes at him in a scowl.

'That is a rude thing to say,' the little man replied. 'I could take offense.'

Perhaps sensing he was not in a position of strength here; Rick didn't bite at the barely concealed threat. Instead, he said, 'Look, the lady said no thank you. We have other places to be, so we'll be on our way.' He shook his arm free and the man let it go but held his position blocking our path.

I thought the greasy-looking man in his cheap suit was going to hit Rick, so I stepped in quickly, distracting him with a question of my own. 'Perhaps you can help us,' I said. 'We are looking for two friends of ours. A man and a woman, both very tall and wearing all black clothing with big boots. I believe they came along here just a few minutes ago.'

'Yes, yes,' the man replied, smiling excitedly. 'They are in here waiting for you.' He was pointing to the club again, but this time when I looked the two door guards were no longer there. I didn't believe for one moment that the Brentnalls were actually inside and I wasn't going in to find out.

How did I now say that I didn't believe him though? I didn't have to, of course, because Rick did it for me. 'I think you're full of crap,' he said.

The little man swung his arm back to slap Rick's face, but Barbie caught it before it could connect. The situation was getting increasingly dangerous and there was still no sign of the Brentnalls. In the frozen second that followed, the little man swung his gaze from Rick to Barbie and Akamu made to step between us to rescue his friend, but the two tattooed henchmen appeared from behind us and grabbed him. One man pinning both his arms easily while the other man stepped around me to take up position behind Rick. He had a cleaver hanging from his right hand.

'Look, we don't want any trouble,' said Barbie, trying but failing to keep the nervous tremble from her voice.

The greasy little man lowered his arm as she let go of it, his broken-toothed smile returning. 'You come for a drink now, yes?' It no longer sounded like a request. 'Your friends will be pleased to see you. Right this way.' Then he turned toward the dark entrance and began walking.

We glanced at each other, but I knew we were going inside so I started walking. 'This is an illegal casino,' hissed Rick over my shoulder as he followed close behind. 'We get these in Hawaii, the gangs set them up just as quickly as we can shut them down. They lure tourists in with pretty girls usually and ply them with free drinks before ripping them off.'

I nodded rather than speak. Maybe the Brentnalls were inside. Maybe I would be able to use Rick or Akamu to ask them some innocent sounding questions and find out a little more about what they were up to.

They were not inside though. At least, there was no sign of them. 'Please, sit, sit,' the little man said. The guards came inside with us. Taking up positions just inside the door. It was late morning but there were already people in the horrid little place. Older Japanese men and women were playing a game that looked a lot like bingo, sitting around a table while a young woman in a booth drew cards from a bag and yelled out something that meant something to the players. There were rows of slot machines with people playing them and tables set up for poker and roulette. A pair of overweight American men were playing at one of the poker tables, each of them with a pair of pretty Japanese girls in cocktails dresses paying them too much attention and making sure they had drinks.

I didn't bother to pull the little man up on his lie about the Brentnalls; there seemed no point. My goal was to get out of this place as soon as we could. He led us to the bar where another pretty girl in a blue cocktail dress was pouring drinks. They looked unappealing, much the same as the entire establishment. Getting angry and feeling brave, I tapped greasy man on the shoulder. 'Look, we have other places to be and I need to find our friends. Just tell me how much I need to spend to get out of here.'

He kept his smile in place as he replied, 'You can go now, if you wish. The boss will want to meet this one though,' he said, pointing to Barbie.

'Me, why?' she asked, her brow crinkled. 'What did I do?'

'He will want to offer you a job. You are very sexy white lady. He have lots of money for you.' The little man was leering at her. It was Barbie's nightmare again, the reason she had been reluctant to come ashore here.

'I don't need a job, thank you.' She made her answer sound definite, but the man wasn't listening. He had already turned to motion the doormen across.

When they approached, he spoke to them in Japanese, giving them instructions, then turned back to Barbie. 'You will wait here for the boss. Your friends can go.'

The two thugs moved between us like sheepdogs separating a flock. 'Now hold on a minute,' Rick began saying but both he and Akamu were grabbed by their collars. They might have been strong men in their younger years, but age had robbed them of it, and they were no match for the two large henchmen. Nevertheless, both men started swearing and swatting at the thugs now steering them toward the door.

'You can go too,' the greasy man sneered at me. 'The boss will just want the pretty one with the big boobs.' He then gave Barbie a pat on her rump and that was where it all went wrong.

'You don't get to touch me,' snapped Barbie, spinning around to grab the man's hand. He looked surprised at how fast she moved, but far more surprised when she folded his hand into his arm pit, spun him around and shoved him into the bar. The drinks spilled as his face collided with them, his shout of anger turning the two ugly henchmen around.

They let go of Akamu and Rick to deal with whatever threat the greasy man was shouting about but when they saw that Barbie had him pinned to the bar, they both laughed. Their mirth was short lived though. My elderly friends might not be all that dynamic anymore, but they knew how to take a big man down from behind. As the henchmen laughed at the little man, they both took a step forward to swing a kick out and up. They were almost invisible from where I stood, obscured by the bigger men, but I saw a foot appear between each henchman's legs as their kicks struck home.

It looked like a score for the home team but there was no time for jubilations; they were not the only thugs in the casino. Across the room, two more tattooed henchman dropped what they were doing and began running in our direction.

I yelled, 'Run,' and started shoving Rick toward the door. Behind me Barbie squealed but she caught up to me in two seconds, bounding between us to fling the door open as the henchmen closed in.

'Which way?' she yelled as we hit the street, daylight blinding my eyes to make me squint. To my mind it didn't matter which way we went; I couldn't see how we were going to get away and I heard the doors burst open behind me just as we came through the market stalls and back up to the narrow alley that ran between them.

'Quick, Rick, grab a weapon,' yelled Akamu, pulling a frying pan from the stove top and tipping the contents out so he could brandish it.

Rick looked about as the stall owner began squawking obscenities at Akamu. He tried to grab another pan, but she swung at him with the cleaver she'd been using to cut up fish. So, he grabbed the fish, a small tuna by the look of it, and held it beside his head like a bat in a classic baseball pose.

Akamu looked at his friend and shook his head. 'You are such a let-down,' he sighed.

Then the first pair of thugs, the ones Rick and Akamu kicked in the spuds, pushed their way between the second pair and we were facing four large men all being urged on by the greasy, little toad in his cheap suit. What chance did we stand?

Fear was making my knees feel weak, but as my brain clawed for something I could say to defuse the situation, I heard the sound of running feet. Then a blur leapt over the stall to land in front of Rick and Akamu and before I could blink it had kicked one henchman in the face and was twirling on the spot to deliver a blow to the one next to him.

Barbie touched my arm to pull me away. 'Is that Hideki?' she asked as she tugged me backward. In turn, I grabbed Rick's arm to get him to come with me. I couldn't move though; the display of fighting skills before me was too fascinating to take my eyes away. Hideki ducked beneath a swinging cleaver that should have taken his head off, to then pop back up like a jack in the box. The swinging cleaver carried the man's arm around and brought him off balance because it connected with nothing but thin air. Hideki punched him in the throat then spun and hit the next man, then bounced back and hit the previous one again. He reminded me of a spinning top crossed with a Tasmanian devil. Soon only the greasy little man was standing.

As he came out of a defensive crouch, checking about to make sure all threats were neutralised, Hideki stole a look in our direction. Seeing the four of us watching him he flapped his arms in an exasperated gesture. 'Run?' he suggested. Then, as we started moving, he yelled, 'Hey!' and pointed down the street. 'That way.'

Barbie reacted first, turning around to go the other way and running directly into Akamu who was close behind her. He put his hands up in a natural defensive reaction, catching a handful of boob with each as she bounced off him.

'You might want to hurry?' suggested Hideki as the thugs were starting to get up again. With apologies and red faces, we all managed to get pointed the right way and could finally see Hideki's taxi parked at the end of the street. We were going as fast as we could, which is to say, not very fast at all, because Rick and Akamu's fast shuffle wasn't much different to their normal one.

I could hear our saviour muttering in Japanese as he hurried us along, plipping the car open just before we reached it so we could all pile inside. There were groans from the two older men as they folded themselves into the back seat again, but Hideki wasn't waiting for the doors to shut; the second our bums hit the seats, he mashed the pedal to the floor and we were gone, inertia flinging the doors shut.

In the back of the cab, I opened my mouth to speak. I needed to thank Hideki for saving us, but as I breathed in, I got a taste of something very unpleasant.

Next to me, Rick said, 'Sorry.' He looked very sheepish and his cheeks were colouring.

'Did you fart?' Akamu demanded to know. 'Wow, man, you stink.'

'I don't think breakfast agreed with me,' he replied. 'I don't feel too good.'

I powered down a window to sweep clean air through the cab. Then leaned forward to talk to the driver. 'Hideki that was so brave of you. What made you come back for us?'

He shrugged like it was nothing, but said, 'I thought you might need help. The Zanooza tend to prey on tourists. They see them as easy targets; people with fat wallets that can be easily picked clean.'

Barbie put her hand on his thigh, and I saw him glance down at it and then at her before forcing his eyes back to the road ahead. 'Patty is right, Hideki, that was ever so brave. You took on four men with weapons to save people you don't know.'

'Yeah, well...' he didn't finish the sentence, but he didn't have to. I knew why he had done it. I had seen other men look at Barbie the same way. It wasn't just that she was pretty and had a perfect body, she also had a kind of inner glow that drew people to her. She was beautiful inside and out. Silence settled in the car until Hideki broke it by asking, 'Where to?'

'I think I need to go back to the ship,' said Rick with a groan that suggested he was doing his best to keep any further gas emissions under control.

Hideki looked to me in his rear-view mirror as if I was spokesperson and leader of the team. No one else said anything though; they were all looking at me as well. 'To the ship it is,' I concluded. Perhaps we could regroup and do something else with our afternoon. My quest to save Anna was driven only by a feeling of responsibility or duty to the man I saw take his own life yesterday. I was getting nowhere though. I still didn't even know his name so perhaps I was going to have to accept that I couldn't solve this one. My friends didn't deserve to be dragged along on my adventures anyway. Rick and Akamu were on the trip of a lifetime and so far hadn't been able to see any of the items on their list.

There and then I made the decision to abandon the search for the elusive, unidentified Anna. I would waste no further time on it.

Yeah. That plan lasted about fifteen minutes.

I knew something was wrong before we got out of the car. On the dock by the ship, there were too many of the ship's security team looking altogether too poised for everything to be okay. Not only that, but I counted four police cars parked haphazardly with the cops milling around next to the white uniforms of the ship's crew. As I stepped out of the car and held the door open for Akamu, I spotted someone I knew.

Lieutenant Schneider and I had some history; he had been appointed as personal security for me at one point and had suffered for it, getting tasered by a pair of criminal lowlifes just because he was in my vicinity. He saw me making a beeline for him and left the group he was with to intercept me. 'Mrs Fisher, you are back sooner than I expected. None of the other passengers have returned yet. Is everything okay?'

I offered him a lopsided grin. 'Our morning has been interesting. I think we will head back out once we have had a chance to regroup.' Then I nodded my head toward the assembled security personnel. 'What's going on? Some kind of drill?'

He pursed his lips before he answered. 'That is the official story, yes. The truth though, is that two men pulled weapons on the guard and forced their way onto the ship an hour ago. We have teams looking for them now and extra guards out here in case there are any more. The captain is handling it personally.'

'Goodness. Do you know why they wanted to get aboard?'

'Not yet.'

Barbie arrived with the slow-moving Rick and Akamu. 'What's happening?' she asked.

Lieutenant Schneider shot his eyes at me; he shouldn't have told me and didn't want anyone else to know because a secret shared soon isn't a secret at all. The passengers would not like to hear that the ship was stormed by armed men. I didn't have to answer her with an evasive answer though, Lieutenant Schneider remembered something. 'I should tell you that I believe we identified the man you saw last night.'

I tilted my head – so they had been looking into the man's identity even though they said they weren't. I wondered if Commander Shriver had driven that herself or if someone like Schneider had taken the task on without instruction. 'Who was it?' I asked. Maybe with a name, I would be able to work out who Anna is.

'I need to show you a picture,' he replied, looking behind at the crew so he could signal to someone. I recognised Lieutenant Deepa Bhukari as she separated from the crowd to start in our direction. 'We had a member of crew that didn't report for shift last night. It wasn't reported until this morning, but he matches your description a little too closely for me to believe it is coincidence.'

Deepa arrived looking expectantly at Schneider when he said, 'Do you have your pad with you?' She produced a small electronic tablet from a side pocket on her uniform shorts and handed it over. Schneider fiddled with it then turned it to face me. 'Is this the man you saw?'

It was a head shot, the sort that human resources would take for a personnel file, but the man was smiling in it and looked vastly different to the poor wretch I met just a few hours ago. It was the same man though. I nodded. 'That's him. Who was he?'

Schneider handed the tablet back to Deepa but she stayed with us as he explained. 'His name is Riku Takahashi. He worked in the engine room as a mechanic. He was a new member of crew, with us for just over seven months and was recruited right here in Tokyo.'

Taking that information in, I asked, 'Has anyone looked into the connection with anyone called Anna?'

Barbie and the others were listening to our exchange, but Rick looked uncomfortable. 'I really need to get back to my cabin,' he said while holding his belly.

'I will have guards escort you,' Schneider said, turning to look beyond Deepa to the group of guards near the ship's entrance.

Barbie interrupted. 'Whoa. Why would we need an escort?'

'A minor security issue,' he replied dismissively, trying to keep a lid on the truth. He called two men over, giving them instruction on what to do before sending them away with Rick and Akamu. I promised to catch up with them later, choosing to stay with Schneider because I could feel the pull of the mystery and I hadn't received an answer to my question about Anna.

Barbie stayed with me, and once our two elderly friends had shuffled away, she leaned in closer to Schneider and Bhukari. 'Seriously, what is going on that we have to send passengers on board with an armed guard?' she whispered.

Schneider sighed and explained about the two men that forced their way on board. This time though he added an extra piece of information; a description. The men were tattooed.

'What did the tattoos look like?' I asked, bringing his attention back to me.

He gave me a dumbfounded look. 'Um.'

Helping him out, I asked, 'Did they have a tattoo on their necks in the shape of a dragon's skull with a rat poking out of the left eye socket?' He didn't know but using his radio he soon got an answer. 'Then they are Zanooza,' I told him, wondering what it meant that they wanted to get on board so desperately that they would risk incarceration or worse.

Frowning, Schneider asked, 'How do you know that, Mrs Fisher?'

My lopsided grin returned as I reminded him, 'We had an interesting morning.' Then I changed the subject back to the question I wanted answered, 'Did anyone look into a connection between Riku and someone called Anna?'

Barbie moved closer to hear his answer. 'I did it myself. But I couldn't find anyone by that name. He does have a wife listed in his personnel file, but her name is Aiko. They have no children thankfully and Commander Shriver is on her way to the address listed for her now. She said that it was her task to let the next of kin know and it wasn't a subject to be disclosed over the phone.' I remembered what Rick and Akamu said earlier about delivering notice of death to relatives. I wanted to talk to his wife but to do so I would almost certainly need a translator.

Then I had a thought. 'Do you have an address for her?'

Schneider looked surprised at the question. 'I don't,' he stammered, then turned to look at Deepa who was already pulling the small tablet from her pocket again.

This time she didn't hand it over but looked up the information herself. 'It's not listed,' she said, but her fingers continued to tap away on the screen for a few seconds until she stopped and turned it to face me. 'Here you go. She lives just outside Tokyo in a small place, at least it looks like a small place on the map, called Yummemigasaki.'

'Is there a phone number?' asked Barbie.

Schneider shook his head. 'No, Commander Shriver set off in one of the cars not that long ago. That's why the captain is handling the security issue personally.'

I wriggled my nose as I made a decision, then turned to Barbie, caught myself before I spoke and checked across to the line of taxis. Hideki's car was still there, close to the back of the short line. Unlike this morning, when there were probably over a hundred cars lining up to take people places, now that all the passengers were gone, I could count only six cars and his was number five. 'Do you fancy a trip through the countryside?' I asked Barbie.

'Now?'

I shrugged at her. 'I figure today is a bust already. It's too late to go anywhere like Mount Fuji, which I know the guys plan to visit on the coach tomorrow, and I really don't feel like heading back into Tokyo itself, I had enough of that this morning.'

'Me too,' she echoed.

'So, I think I will have Hideki take me for a drive to see the poor widow. Commander Shriver will have told her by the time we arrive, and I really just want to ask her about Anna. It's my last-ditch attempt to find out who it was that he wanted me to save. No one else is trying to solve the riddle of his death.' It felt like I had just insulted Schneider and Bhukari but neither reacted, perhaps silently agreeing that the ship's security was not viewing it as a priority. No one but me had heard his plea after all.

Barbie gave it a moment's thought, but smiled and said, 'Yeah, sure, Patty. That sounds great.'

60

I nodded at Schneider and Bhukari as we turned to head back to the taxi rank, then stopped. 'Can you write down that address for me?' I asked, then waited while Deepa wrote it into a notebook and tore off the page. I was sure Rick and Akamu would forgive us for taking off without them. I wasn't sure Rick would be up to doing much today anyway.

As we walked toward the taxi, Hideki, who appeared to be singing along to the radio, spotted us coming and smiled as he turned it down. 'I think he likes you,' I said and bumped Barbie's hip with mine as we walked.

She giggled. 'I kind of like him. He is ever so handsome, and I got a bit hot watching him fight those men earlier. It was ever so impressive the way he dealt with them.'

Further conversation ceased as we arrived at his car. He powered the driver's window down to talk to us. 'Have you not had enough adventure for one day, ladies?'

'Almost,' I replied with a smile. I showed him the address. 'Can you take us there?'

He took the page and I watched as his lips moved a little while he read. 'Sure. What's there though? This is way outside the city.'

All the cool air-conditioned air was escaping through his window and it was a swelteringly hot day. I grabbed the door handle. 'We'll explain on the way.'

Barbie and I shared the backseat, this time with plenty of room instead of cramped like we had been this morning. Hideki stopped at a sushi joint on the road which he claimed served the best Gukan-Maki anywhere in Japan and then admitted that it was his uncle's joint when I insisted he let me pick up the bill. He was right about the food though; it was wonderful and plentiful and unbelievably fresh.

Not including the stop for lunch, the journey took just over an hour which he said was only because it was the right time of day to be heading this way. If we hung about too long, the trip back to the dock would be much slower as traffic through the city would snarl up. He agreed to translate for us and during the drive we chatted amiably back and forth which is how we found out he was driving the cab while studying to be a doctor. This was his final year of school and soon he would take up a position in a hospital. He planned to go to America which was why he paid so much attention to his English.

Arriving finally at the address for Mrs Takahashi, I could see one of the ship's limousines parked outside. The cruise line owned a number of them, so they had them waiting at each port and I could have called on one of them myself had I wanted to; it was a perk I enjoyed as a guest in a Royal Suite. This morning had been so hurried with me chasing after the Brentnalls that I hadn't had a chance to consider it. Looking back though, the enormous black car would have stuck out badly had we ridden in that and there would have been no Hideki to come to our rescue.

The presence of the limousine here meant that Commander Shriver was still inside. I briefly considered waiting around the corner until she was gone, but it felt cowardly, so I prepared myself to deal with the hard-to-like woman and set off for the house.

With Barbie and Hideki at my side, I knocked on the door and stepped back to wait. A Japanese woman in her late thirties answered, but if I had expected a grieving widow or even a tearful other close relative that might have been called upon to visit and give comfort, I was to be denied. Instead, the lady at the door looked more bored than anything.

She addressed us in Japanese and though I didn't understand it, I was fairly certain she had not just said hello. Hideki responded, the exchange of words lasting no more than a few seconds before she stepped back to allow us in.

Hideki said, 'Mrs Takahashi welcomes you to her humble abode.' I didn't think she had said that at all, but I kept quiet as I stepped inside. Were we supposed to remove our shoes? I had a feeling we were but couldn't remember what the correct etiquette was in different cultures, plus globalisation was changing what newer generations thought was acceptable. I got inside and stopped until I could see what Hideki would do, then followed his lead as he stripped off his footwear.

Mrs Takahashi led us through to a quiet room which contained books and plants but no television. Commander Shriver was sitting in an armchair. She did not look pleased to see me. 'Why are you here?' she asked before I had a chance to speak.

Rather than answer her question, which I thought a little rude, I spoke to Hideki, 'Can you please ask Mrs Takahashi if she knows of anyone called Anna or believes that her husband would know of anyone by that name.'

He nodded, turned to the woman and translated my question. Mrs Takahashi began talking at a fast rate. For several minutes. Hideki mostly listened, but once or twice he said. 'Hai.' Or asked what I thought was a qualifying question to check on a particular point. When she finally stopped talking, Hideki turned back to us and said, 'Mrs Takahashi filed for divorce almost a year ago and has no idea who Anna might be.'

I waited for more and when it became apparent that there was nothing further to come, I said, 'That's it? All that stuff she just said, and it translated to she's getting divorced and doesn't know anyone called Anna?'

Hideki nodded his head smartly as if congratulating himself for a job well done. 'She also said that Anna might be some new girlfriend, but she doesn't care. He can go burn in hell.' Righto. Mrs Takahashi wasn't overly bothered about her husband's death then.

Commander Shriver, bored with being ignored, left her chair to join the conversation. 'This is none of your business, Mrs Fisher,' she advised, keeping her tone neutral so it just sounded like she was being friendly or helpful.

Without looking at her I replied, 'No. It's yours.' And left it at that, my thoughts on her lack of activity thus far quite clear.

Barbie asked, 'Did she say why they were getting a divorce?'

Hideki smiled again. 'Ah, yes, she did. She called him a worthless piece of… crap, I think is the direct translation. A gambling addict moron who squandered all of their money and left her in debt before he ran away to the sea to escape the Zanooza.'

Bing! Just like that we had a big fat clue. He had been terrified yesterday, determined that killing himself was the only solution. They would kill him tomorrow if he didn't do it for them today. That was what he said.

'Ask her if the Zanooza were after him because of gambling debt?' Hideki looked from me to Mrs Takahashi and started speaking in Japanese again.

Commander Shriver squinted her eyes at me though. 'What is it you hope to achieve, Mrs Fisher? The poor man is dead. Any debt he had went to the grave with him. If they were going to take it from his estranged wife, they would have done it already. What mystery are you trying to solve this time?'

It irked me that she didn't seem to remember about the man's plea to save Anna, but then I remembered that I hadn't told her. I told Baker last night but that didn't mean the message had been passed to her. 'Before Riku jumped, he gave me a piece of paper on which was written the number 2124 and he asked me to save Anna. I don't know who Anna is, but I intend to find out. Will you help me?'

The thin, odd-looking woman gave me a quizzical look, weighing up my explanation before saying, 'It seems I have misunderstood your intentions, Mrs Fisher. I apologise if I came across as harsh.' She didn't expand on her statement, but I shook her hand when she extended it and it felt like we were starting over again. 'What have you been able to find out so far?'

'Not very much. Mostly I have been eliminating leads which proved to be dead ends. I think he was involved with the couple in cabin 2124. I don't suppose you are familiar with them, but they look like a very nasty pair and when I spoke with them last night, their instant reaction was to threaten me. We followed them to a very seedy part of Tokyo today but lost them when we got caught at some lights. They got out though and they are up to something. I think that had something to do with Riku's death, but I don't yet know how they are connected.'

'What makes you so sure they are connected?'

'The note. Why else would he give me the number of their cabin?' Commander Shriver didn't have an answer but I could see she was giving it some thought.

Hideki was done conversing with Mrs Takahashi and was waiting for my attention before he updated me. 'Mrs Takahashi says the Zanooza came here looking for something. They took what money she had and trashed the place looking for whatever it was, but they didn't find it. They didn't tell her what it was either, only that it was important and was a personal possession of Mr Tanaka.'

'Who is Mr Tanaka?' asked Barbie.

With a serious face, Hideki said, 'He's the kingpin of the Tokyo underworld and the leader of the Zanooza. If Riku Takahashi took something from him, he was as good as dead. Handing it back wouldn't have saved him. It would be a matter of honour that he be punished.'

It was Commander Shriver's turn to ask a question. 'Why take it then?' She wasn't asking Hideki though, there was no way for him to answer her. The question was aimed at all of us. It was a good question. Riku had taken something from the boss of a Tokyo organised crime gang and had done so on top of running up insurmountable gambling debt. A better question might be why he didn't get off the ship in any one of the other ports the ship stopped at. He hadn't though and now he never would.

I could see nothing further to be gained by spending any further time with Mrs Takahashi, so we thanked her for her time and departed, stopping only to put our shoes back on. Just as I got outside her door, a thought occurred to me. 'Hideki?'

'Yes, ma'am?'

'Can you ask Mrs Takahashi one last question?' I was already pushing him back through the door he had been exiting. Mrs Takahashi flared her eyes in frustration but did her best to level an expression of toleration. 'Please ask her if 2124 means anything to her?'

He complied, but her perplexed frown preceded a head shake: she had no idea what the number might mean in conjunction with her dead husband. Disappointed, but not surprised, I finally left the poor woman alone.

Outside, Commander Shriver, who I hoped I might now get on with a little better, slid into her limousine and left, her driver prescribing a wide arc as he swung the large car around to face back toward Tokyo. Hideki, Barbie, and I followed close behind in his taxi. It was the middle of the afternoon and there was plenty of day left for other activities, but I felt that I was done for the day.

Barbie said the same thing, stifling a yawn with one hand as she did. We travelled in silence for a while and I stared out the window at the scenery flashing by. Tomorrow, I would be a tourist and travel with Rick and Akamu to Mount Fuji. There were coaches leaving from the dockside at something like eight o'clock in the morning. They needed to leave at that time because of the distance involved, but the ship was due to depart twelve hours after that at eight o'clock in the evening and there would be no more time to solve the riddle of Anna and what she needed to be saved from.

Despite my renewed excitement after discovering the man's name, I was no closer to learning anything pertinent. Anna wasn't his wife and Anna didn't appear to be known by anyone connected to him. I was going to have to face facts and let it go.

Feeling like a failure, I turned my thoughts to gin. Whenever I felt down, gin could always be my friend, but this time, when I thought about a nice cold crisp glass of gin, I remembered drinking one with the captain. It was more than one actually and we had talked for hours as I got to know him, and he got to know me.

He had never been married, something he said he regretted, and at the time I couldn't help thinking he was telling me that for a reason. I was a little tipsy at the time and dismissed the notion once I sobered up, but more than once that night and since, he expressed a desire to get to know me better and suggested we have a private dinner together.

Remembering that now, I took out my phone and typed him a text message. My finger hovered over the send button for several seconds as I debated with myself about sending it. Then remembered the promise I made to myself: I was a new woman, with a new life and a whole new outlook. I wasn't the mousy invisible speck I had been. I was a lioness now and I was going to roar.

I jabbed the send button with a determined thumb and spent the rest of the journey alternately berating myself for doing so and congratulating myself for being brave.

Little did I know the surprise waiting for me on board the ship.

Despite staring at my phone and daring it to beep with a new message, I made it all the way back to my suite without the captain answering my dinner invitation. I kept telling myself he was probably too busy to read personal messages and it had only been an hour. Even so, I had to assume he wasn't coming. Like a teenage schoolgirl, in the car I checked my phone every few seconds, willing him to answer either way and believing he would join me if he could. My message had been a simple one and quite nonchalant in its wording.

Please join me for dinner in my suite at eight if you are able. I shall hope to see you then. Patricia

That he had given me the number for his personal phone had to mean something. I didn't know what it meant and I wasn't sure what I wanted it to mean. However, I had to admit that I was drawn to him in a way that I hadn't been drawn to a man since I met Charlie more than three decades ago. Alistair Huntley was handsome and athletic, and he was a delight to talk to, always taking an interest in whoever he met. I knew that, in theory, I was still married to Charlie, but emotionally, I had already moved on. Could I have another relationship at my age? Was that a thing? The concept made me nervous. Extremely nervous. But it also filled me with hope. What would it be like to kiss Alistair Huntley? Could I?

All these thoughts raged through my head as I walked from the elevator to my door. I needed a shower and I needed a gin. I checked my phone one more time as I pushed the door open with my hip, then seeing the unread message count was still zero, I dropped it sullenly into my handbag and walked into my living area.

Then, the keycard I placed between my lips to leave my hands free for phone fiddling, dropped from my mouth as my jaw fell open.

Standing in the middle of my living area, right between the two couches arranged there, was my husband.

He heard me coming in and had stood up to greet me. I was too stunned to speak though and stared at him mutely, hoping I would blink and he wouldn't be there at all.

'Patricia, darling,' he gushed as he crossed the room to get to me, his arms out wide to wrap me into a hug.

That got me moving. 'Charlie, what on earth are you doing here?' If the question wasn't enough to halt his advance, the warning hand I held up was.

'I came to be with you, darling. You always wanted me to take a cruise with you, so here I am. I have missed you so terribly.'

'Maggie not much of a cook then?' I shot back. We were standing no more than four feet apart and I could smell his old familiar aftershave. It was a comforting smell somehow, but the sense of betrayal still controlled my tongue.

Charlie hung his head in shame, staring at the carpet when he said, 'Let's not fight, darling. I couldn't be more sorry. I can't undo it now, but I can live my life trying to make amends.' He looked back up. 'I bought you flowers.'

I looked to where he was pointing on the coffee table behind him. A sensible sized bunch of oriental lilies in a spray was sitting in a vase. I realised then that I had detected the smell when I came through the door but thought nothing of it because Jermaine ensured there were fresh cut flowers every few days. Then a thought occurred to me. 'How did you get on board?'

Charlie seemed to relax at that point, as if me asking a question that wasn't about his infidelity somehow meant I was over it. He turned and walked back to the couches, sitting in one and crossing his legs as he got comfortable. 'I had to um... sweet talk my way on board. My flight got in early this morning but not early enough to catch you before you left for the day. Where have you been anyway?' he asked, then seeing my expression, he flapped a dismissive hand. 'Nevermind. Not important. So, anyway, I spoke with the ship's security and they had to make some calls so they could verify my identity. It took a while, but once I showed them our marriage certificate and they were satisfied that I was joining you for the rest of the cruise, they escorted me up here.' He gestured around the suite. 'I must say, it is not what I expected. I figured you would be in a tiny cabin somewhere below decks. The fellow that brought me up here had two men to carry my bags and he told me this is the best suite on the ship.'

I just stared at him in disbelief still trying to wrap my head around the fact that he was on board in the first place.

He kept on talking though, just like he always did at home, never letting me get a word in and not interested in anything I might have to say. 'Tell me, darling. How is it that you are affording this palatial suite? Is this what you did with the money you took from my accounts?'

'Our accounts,' I snapped in reply.

He held up a hand in surrender. 'Yes, yes. Our accounts.' He fell silent for a second, but I knew he had more to say. 'It was my money though, Patricia. It was me that had to earn it. Your meagre income couldn't support a hamster at harvest time. I know you were angry at me but this...' He waved his arm around to indicate the room again. 'Shouldn't we move to a more sensibly priced cabin for the rest of the trip?'

I couldn't believe him. I just couldn't. I opened my mouth to speak, felt the anger rising and bit it back down, turning on my heel as I went to my bedroom. I needed a shower, so that was what I was going to do next. I would deal with Charlie once I felt a little less scuzzy.

I stayed in the shower for far longer than was necessary, finally emerging when my skin was starting to wrinkle, and I stayed in my room after that. In the end, I left the privacy and solitude of my bedroom because it was starting to feel like I was hiding in there. Walking back into the living area, there was no sign of Charlie, but Jermaine was in the kitchen. He looked to be preparing dinner.

He said, 'Good evening, madam,' as I approached.

I returned his salutation and accepted the gin and tonic gratefully. He and I had fallen into a happy routine over the last few weeks, so he knew when to have a gin ready for me. Today the gin was necessary. I gulped a mouthful of the cold liquid before I asked him, 'Where is he?' I didn't need to say who *he* was; it was obvious enough.

He flicked his eyes toward the glass doors that led out to my private sun terrace. Charlie was leaning against the railing, looking out to sea. We were still in dock of course so the scene outside was set and only the slight breeze borne on the natural air currents was ruffling his hair. I downed my glass, barely acknowledging the harsh hit of alcohol, then, still staring at my husband and wondering what would happen if I just shoved him over the side, I asked Jermaine for another.

I didn't need to see it to know that he flared his eyes in surprise when he took a fresh glass from the cupboard and made me a second drink. 'Has he spoken to you?' I asked.

Jermaine's wonderfully deep voice answered, 'Yes, madam.' He left it at that though, making me work for more information.

72

'What did he say to you, please?'

Jermaine sighed quietly, an involuntary gesture he tried to hide. 'He refers to me as *the help*.' That sounded about right. Charlie wasn't much of a people person. He didn't even know the name of his own secretary; he kept referring to her as Barbara when her name was Michelle. Just then he turned and spotted me inside. A smile lit his face and he immediately started back toward me.

Coming through the doors, he was speaking before he was fully inside. 'Patricia, dear. I thought we might have dinner in here tonight. Something intimate; just the two of us, you know. I'm sure the help can put something together for us.'

'Do you mean my butler, Jermaine?' I asked, fixing him with a hard stare. 'Jermaine is an accomplished chef among other skills. So, yes, let's have dinner together and a proper conversation about the divorce and how we now split our assets. There's no reason why we cannot do this amicably.'

Charlie's smile didn't even crack. 'There's no reason why we need to do it at all, darling. Come. Let's sit and discuss all things us. Jeremy, can you bring some wine? Something cold, bold, and fruity, if you please.' He walked to the couches, offering his hand to take, but retracting it when I didn't. 'Getting divorced makes no financial sense in the current climate, Patricia. Why don't you come and sit with me while I explain it?'

I felt my back teeth grind together and my top lip twitch but a knock at the door disturbed my murderous train of thought. Jermaine stopped what he was doing, removed the apron he always wore when working in the kitchen and crossed the room at his usual dignified butler's pace.

My brain wasn't firing on all cylinders because Charlie's arrival had thrown me completely off balance. Had I been thinking straight I would have known who the caller at my door was before he came into the room.

'Good evening, Patricia. I trust you were able to explore Tokyo today. I'm sorry I wasn't able to join...' Captain Alistair Huntley stopped mid-sentence as he saw the other man in my suite. 'I'm terribly sorry,' he said, addressing Charlie. 'I don't believe we have been introduced.' He entered the suite with a bouquet of roses (my favourite) in his hands but handed them to Jermaine as he doffed his hat. As Jermaine took the long route around the room, silently ignoring the stand-off about to occur, Alistair stepped forward to offer Charlie his hand. 'Good evening, I'm Alistair Huntley, the captain of this fine vessel and...'

'And a hound, sir!' snapped Charlie, standing up once more to confront what he perceived to be his rival. 'Why are you here this evening, sir? Do you have plans for my wife?' Alistair clearly hadn't known about Charlie's arrival and for the first time since I met him, he was lost for words and looked genuinely confused. He was looking directly at Charlie who had bunched his fists and was managing to look angry. Or as angry as a balding actuary can manage to look.

I stepped in. 'Charlie, this is my friend, Alistair. He is the captain of this ship and a lot has happened since I came on board.' I was about to explain about the deputy captain and the mobsters and that I had invited Alistair for dinner tonight and then forgotten I had done so because Charlie's unexpected arrival wiped my brain clean. I didn't get to though because Charlie went nuts.

'What!? You're sleeping with him!? You have the nerve to berate me for an infidelity that you pushed me to, when all the while you are here in bed with another man?'

'You will lower your tone and watch your manners, sir,' Alistair insisted, bristling at Charlie's impertinence.

I wasn't about to let Alistair get into a fight with Charlie over me. I intended to get rid of Charlie before we set sail tomorrow, which I was sure would mean talking some sense into him. To do that, I needed him calm and alone. So, I stepped in between the two men, my back to Charlie as I addressed the captain. With imploring and apologetic eyes, I said, 'I need some time alone with my husband, Alistair. Can you grant me that for now, please?'

It took him no more than a second to regain his composure, visibly straightening himself as he forced all the anger from his face. 'Of course, Mrs Fisher.' He looked beyond me to acknowledge Charlie. 'Good evening, Mr Fisher.' Jermaine had already moved to the door to let the captain out and the situation was defused.

Charlie had to have the last word though; petty to the end. 'Don't let the door hit your arse on the way out,' he shouted just as Alistair departed. I turned to face him rather than continue staring longingly at the door and saw his triumphant smile.

I slapped his face.

I hit him hard enough to make my hand sting, the sound drawing Jermaine's attention instantly. He had been crossing the room again, heading back to the kitchen when the noise brought him to a halt. A few feet away, he waited patiently and calmly in case there was need to step in. Charlie made no attempt to return the blow though. If anything, he looked embarrassed that *the help* had witnessed it. His expression was wounded though as he rubbed at his cheek.

'I am going to bed,' I announced. 'Jermaine, would you be so kind as to make up a light meal for me? A salad perhaps with some salmon. Provide

75

for Mr Fisher only if you wish to.' As Jermaine nodded his head and continued toward the kitchen, I turned my attention to Charlie.

'What has gotten into you, Patricia?' he asked. 'I barely recognise you. You have lost weight, which to be fair was long overdue. Your hair is different, you have clearly been wasting money on clothes and you have thrown away a good portion of our life savings on a ridiculous holiday of a lifetime. When are you going to stop?'

I made a hmming noise as I thought about his question. 'When am I going to stop? Which bit of it are you referring to, I wonder, because the answer to every element is never. Oh, I'll return to England when all this is done. But you are going to have to accept that our marriage is over, Charlie.' I said it as kindly as I could. I didn't wish him ill, though I felt that I would be well within my rights to. I just wanted to move on.

He wasn't getting it though. He dropped the hand that had been rubbing his cheek and shot me a smile. 'Then I shall make it my mission to win you back. Starting tomorrow, I will be the most charming version of myself you ever met. We shall spend the day in any way that you wish, and I will be your loving husband from sun up to sun down.'

I stared at him for several seconds, trying to form a new sentence in my head that would get the message across. Nothing came. So, I spoke to Jermaine instead, 'Add several gin and tonics to my dinner order, please.' I made a mental note to hit the gym early so I could burn off the alcohol I now planned to imbibe, but I figured I needed it.

As I walked to my bedroom and shut the door, I told myself he would be gone tomorrow. I was starting to wonder if I might be wrong about that though and what I could do about it if he insisted on staying. A naughty voice from somewhere inside my head told me I could always just throw myself at Alistair, cast my knickers aside and get rid of Charlie by moving into the captain's private quarters. Was it bad that I felt sorely tempted to do just that?

Returning to my suite from the gym the following morning, I heard what I could only describe as a ruckus coming from inside. It was loud enough that I could hear it before I got the door open which was when I saw what was causing it: It was Charlie.

Jermaine had positioned himself like a barrier between two opposing factions and was doing his best to keep them apart. Charlie on one side, was throwing insults and curses at Rick and Akamu on the other. Neither party was doing much to get to the other though. In the case of Rick and Akamu, that was probably in deference to their age. In Charlie's case, it was because all he ever did was make noise; there was never any action.

I sighed deeply as I put my bag down. 'Gentlemen,' I called loudly enough to get their attention. 'What seems to be the problem?' The squabbling ceased as all four men turned their eyes to me.

I would have bet all the money in my safe that it would be Charlie to speak first, and, of course, it was. 'These two men were in your room this morning when I came out for breakfast. They claim to know you and to be working on some kind of secret mission for you.' He said it as if it was the most ludicrous thing he had ever heard.

'Yes,' I replied. 'What of it?' As his mouth flapped in confusion, I looked at my two elderly friends. 'Hey, guys. Do you have something to report?'

Akamu took a pace toward me, 'Yes, I can report that Rick stank out the whole cabin, so I went to stakeout the Brentnalls.'

'It wasn't that bad,' Rick whined.

Charlie was shaking his head in disbelief, 'Stakeout? The Brentnalls? Just what the heck is going on here?'

'It's like we told you,' said Rick. 'Your wife is a super sleuth. She has mad detective skills the rest of us can only dream about.' Then he swung his attention to me. 'You didn't say your husband was joining you.'

I didn't get to comment on his observation of course, because Charlie was talking again. 'A detective?' He forced a fake laugh. 'Don't make me laugh, chaps. Patricia is a cleaner. She scrubs other people's houses for a living. She can't solve a crossword puzzle.'

'What were you able to find out?' I asked, my question aimed at Rick and Akamu while I deliberately ignored Charlie. I distinctly remembered his promise to spend today wooing me, but I wasn't going to remind him about that.

Akamu grimaced as he replied. 'Nothing, actually. I don't think they even came back to the ship. Between us, we watched their door for hours, but they didn't show at any point.'

'Will somebody tell me what is going on?' Charlie demanded angrily. I thought he might stamp his foot if we continued to ignore him and I was fine with that but Akamu tried to explain it to him one more time.

'A man committed suicide but handed Patricia a note before he did. The note gave us the cabin number of the couple that caused him to take his own life.'

'Yeah, and he said he had to kill himself now or they would do it tomorrow,' added Rick, taking over the narrative.

I finished with the final point though, 'Then he begged me to save Anna and jumped off the back of the ship with a weight tied around his waist.'

Charlie was pulling a face that said he could barely believe a word of what he was hearing. 'Okay, so who is Anna and why did he give the note to you?'

'We don't know who Anna is. I haven't been able to work that bit out yet.'

'Some sleuth,' he quipped, and I felt like slapping his face again. This was typical Charlie, just the way he had been for years. Oh, he had been charming when we first met and for the first few years of marriage, so far as I could remember, but he had grown bored of me at some point, his compliments turning to criticisms and then the criticisms becoming more frequent until that was all there was. There had been nothing forcing me to put up with it though. That I had done so was on me.

Ignoring him yet again, I asked, 'Are we still on for the Mount Fuji trip today?' My friends looked at each other, possibly each confirming they had no other plan. 'Jolly good, then. The coaches leave at eight o'clock. Have you had breakfast already?' I glanced at the clock; it was just about to turn seven, so we had plenty of time. 'Jermaine makes a wonderful eggs Benedict if you fancy that?'

'What's at Mount Fuji?' asked Charlie.

Akamu spared him a glance and a curled lip that went with the stupid question. 'A mountain?' he drawled. 'Great views? Clean air? It's a famous mountain.' He shot me a look as if to say, *'What's with this guy?'* but he didn't say it. What he said was, 'I think we'll meet you at the coach.' It was clear to me they would have stayed if my idiot husband wasn't here to ruin things.

Jermaine moved to the door to let them out and I cut my eyes at Charlie to make sure he didn't have some clever last-minute quip to throw at their backs.

80

'You're not really going to look at a mountain, are you?' he asked.

'Yes. I'm going with my friends, but you absolutely don't have to. Perhaps you should pack your bags and look for a flight home. I don't want you hanging around, ruining the remainder of my cruise.'

'Don't be silly, Patricia. We are going to have a wonderful time. We have just been apart a little too long, that's all. We probably need to reacquaint ourselves with each other, that's all. Tell you what; I'll come on the trip today and we will have a lovely time. You can prove me wrong about how interesting it is to look at a really big rock and then, this evening, we can have an intimate dinner in one of the wonderful restaurants. My treat. And then perhaps we take a bottle of champagne into the bedroom and see if we can't put all of this behind us.'

I didn't have to fake throwing up in my mouth because I actually did it. The concept was vile. I couldn't speak for fear I might actually vomit and then Jermaine would have to summon some poor cleaner to deal with it. Charlie was still talking, unconcerned about my response, so I turned on my heel and made sure my bedroom door was locked. I needed to get a shower after my workout and didn't want Charlie to get any ridiculous ideas.

Despite repeated attempts to put him off, Charlie came with me anyway. Upon his insistence, I said, 'Jermaine, have you seen Mount Fuji?' already knowing he had not because the subject was discussed a few days ago.

'I have not, madam.'

'Won't you please accompany me today then? I would hate for you to be stuck on the ship when there is no need.' If Charlie wanted to complain, he didn't, though I saw his hopeful expression slip a little. He was trying to be sweet to me this morning, something he hadn't bothered with in years and had the look of a hurt puppy this morning because nothing he tried was working. When I came out of my bedroom for breakfast, he greeted me with a cup of tea he made himself. He pulled out my chair so I could sit. I saw them as the actions of a desperate man and knew they wouldn't last, his natural character would resurface soon enough. But I guess his evening had involved some soul searching and he was trying to be a husband even though I considered it to all be in vain.

He chatted away on the ride down to the exit, talking about work and a new merger with a Dutch firm currently being considered. He even pointed out that they had let him take all the holiday time he wanted because year after year he failed to take all his assigned vacation days. I shot him a look but he completely missed the irony of his statement and I let him prattle on while I ground my teeth at all the years we had gone to Cornwall instead of exploring the world.

Rick and Akamu were waiting near the coaches but I merely waved at them, opting to keep Charlie away from anyone I knew. The coach was just like any other luxury coach, which is to say that it was comfortable, but not so comfortable that one would want to spend hours on it, which is what we were doing. It was also full, so Charlie and I had to sit together. I tolerated about five minutes of his attempts to engage me in conversation before I said I was tired and feigned sleep. After a while I didn't have to feign it as the gentle rocking motion soothed me into a dreamless doze.

When I awoke, Charlie was also asleep, his head back and his mouth hanging open, though thankfully he wasn't snoring. I twisted carefully in my sleep to find Jermaine behind me. He was sitting next to a small American lady with tight curls in her white hair. She was one of a trio of widows on a trip together and came from somewhere in Nevada. I met them more than a week ago but couldn't now remember their names. She waved a quick hello but saw it was the large black man next to her that I wanted.

I caught his eye. 'Is everything alright, madam?'

I grimaced and nodded my head in Charlie's direction. 'Could be better.'

He had no reply for that, so asked a question. 'Will he be remaining on board until you return to England?'

It was a good question. It was the right question to ask and the answer was no, but I hadn't worked out what I was going to do if he refused to leave. He didn't need a ticket because I had rented the suite. If I complained to the crew, who did I complain to? The captain? Asking the crew to remove my husband because he cheated on me a while ago and I had left him did not feel like a viable option. No, it was on me to get the message across and I had a limited window in which to do it, or we would sail tonight with him still on board.

All I offered Jermaine was a shrug before I turned back to face the right way. Thankfully, my nap eroded most of the journey and we were nearly there, the mountain looming large in front of us. Charlie was still asleep

83

when the coach pulled to a halt and had I been sitting in the aisle seat I would have left him there. I wasn't though and he woke when I tried to climb over him.

'What are you doing, darling? You weren't trying to leave me sleeping on the coach, were you?'

'I was actually.' The truth was the best option; I had no desire to spare his feelings.

He just chuckled though. 'Naughty girl. Always the joker.' Then slid from his seat and started down the coach toward the door.

As I followed him, edging between the seats, I spotted a pair of men looking into the coach from outside. I didn't think they could see through the windows very well, but it was clear they were looking for someone and their standout feature was the Zanooza tattoo each sported. Unsettled by their presence, I told myself it could be nothing but coincidence. When I got outside the coach they had moved on, looking at people disembarking the next coach in line.

'Come along then, darling. Let's explore this mountain,' said Charlie as he crooked his arm to offer me his elbow. I rolled my eyes and moved away, catching up with Rick and Akamu as they shuffled along with the line of passengers wending their way toward the guest centre. At the head of each group was a tour guide, jabbering away about what we were seeing. The first stop today was a pair of lava caves. The group paused while the tour guide explained how they were formed several million years ago, but then stepped aside so everyone could explore by themselves.

Jermaine caught me glancing around behind the group. 'Is everything alright, madam?'

The two thugs I saw earlier were nowhere in sight. I flicked my eyes to take in Jermaine's concerned face. 'Did you really need to wear the butler's uniform today?'

'I am here as your butler, madam.' He seemed to think that was sufficient explanation, so I left it at that to head inside the cool cavern. Charlie was waiting for me at the mouth of the cave where a lady was handing out headsets that would explain the history and religious significance of the caves in more than a dozen different languages. I placed mine on my head and found the audio was triggered as I stepped over a bar on the floor. Walking around the cave, the narration was so intuitive, that it knew where I was and told me about the different formations in that area. The cave was lit in various colours and all quite fascinating, but it did mean that I was listening to the recorded voice and couldn't hear the Zanooza thugs sneaking up behind me until one stuck a gun in my back.

I jumped at the unexpected presence so close to me but a huge hand on my left shoulder held me in place as his colleague did the same to Charlie.

Charlie tried to turn to see who had touched him. 'What the devil?' he exclaimed but the large man behind him spat a reply in Japanese and I saw Charlie react in pain as the gun's muzzle was dug into his ribs.

I glanced about for Jermaine, but couldn't see him, the two men had carefully selected their ambush point and waited until Charlie and I had wandered away from the main body of tourists. Then a voice I recognised said, 'Hello, lady. Where is your pretty friend?' It was the greasy little man in the cheap suit from yesterday.

The thug holding my shoulder wheeled me around to face him and shoved me forward, his gun dug in under my ribs. We were being taken somewhere, the little man neither expecting nor waiting for an answer from me.

'What on earth is going on?' Charlie demanded to know. 'I'll have you know we're British.' I rolled my eyes. Did he really think that having the world's largest empire a hundred years ago made a jot of difference to these men?

'Be quiet, Charlie. They are not about to let us go.'

Ahead of me, the little man stopped walking and turned to face us. 'Actually, I don't think we need the man.' He nodded at the Zanooza thug behind Charlie and mimed cutting a throat with his thumb. 'Do it quietly.'

I sucked in an involuntary gasp of shock as I realised they were just going to kill him now and shook myself free of the thug holding me as I jumped to defend Charlie. 'No! This is my husband. We go together or not at all,' I squealed as I put my arms around him. He might be a terrible husband, but I didn't want to see him have his throat cut. I didn't want anything bad to happen to him, I just wanted him to go home and leave me in peace.

'May I be of assistance, madam?' Jermaine had stepped silently into the small cavern we were being led through and now looked poised, his arms and legs hanging loose and ready to fight.

Yay! Jermaine was going to make them eat their shoes!

Then, a hand appeared behind him with a gun in it. All I could see was the hand, but as more of the person holding it emerged from behind a rock, the gun tapped Jermaine in the back of the head. My spiking adrenaline was making me feel dizzy; were they about to shoot my butler?

Then a fourth Zanooza thug appeared next to the little man, emerging out of the dark from the direction of the exit. The little man reacted to whatever the newest thug said, flapped his arms in annoyance and said, 'We'll take you all, then. Kill you now, kill you later; what's the difference?'

He grinned an evil smile with his terrible teeth, spun on his heel and fell over a rock. The thug behind me started to shove me forward again, but not without a snigger at the little man's misfortune. He was picking himself up and making a racket, swearing no doubt in Japanese as he inspected his suit and found a hole in the knee of his trousers.

Jermaine fell into step beside me, but where he was usually silent and staid and in complete control, right now he was whimpering in fright and wringing his hands. He also sounded far more effeminate than usual. 'Oh, madam, what do they want? Where are they taking us?' Thinking to myself that he never sounded like this, I realised he was acting, trying to make himself appear to be less of a threat.

Charlie didn't get it though. 'Will you shut that wimp up?' he snapped. He didn't say anything else though because the thug to his rear cuffed him in the head with his gun.

Wondering why we hadn't run into any more tourists on the way out, I soon had my answer as the tour guide at the entrance had another pair of Zanooza thugs standing either side of her. There were no fresh coaches in the car park and a pair of black SUVs with blacked out windows were waiting just a few yards away.

I bit down on my rising fear to ask, 'Where are you taking us?' We were about to be put in the cars, there was no one in sight, and even if there had been, no one was coming to save us. I had no idea where we were going or why and I wondered how long it would be before we were reported missing.

The little man, the only one that understood my question, paused beside the passenger door to meet my gaze. 'The boss wants to see you, English lady. He wants to know how you come to be asking questions of Mrs Takahashi. Very pertinent questions about Anna. Maybe if you tell him where it is, he will let you go. Maybe you should tell me where it is right now, and I can be the one to deliver it to him.' He liked that idea, smiling at the thought as if it had just that second occurred to him.

Telling my knees not to buckle, I managed to stammer, 'I don't know what you are talking about.'

'Oh, for goodness sake, Patricia,' snapped Charlie. 'Give them what they want so we can go home. Real home, that is. Not your floating palace sailing toward our utter bankruptcy.'

The little man moved into my personal space. 'You should listen to your husband, Patricia. Give it to me and you can spare yourself a lot of pain. The boss will not ask twice like I have.'

'But I don't know what you are talking about,' I wailed. 'Tell me what it is, and if I have seen it somewhere or know how to find it, I will take you to it.'

'The lion's head. I want the lion's head. Where is it?'

'The lion's head. I don't know what that is.' It was one of those impossible situations that occasionally crop up in life. All you have to do to avoid a terrible event is do one thing, but you can't do that one thing. If I knew what he wanted, I would give it to him without a moment's hesitation.

He pursed his lips in annoyance. 'Have it your way, English lady. I hope you like pain.' His car door slammed as he yanked it closed in anger and a fresh dig in my ribs jolted me back to reality as a thug opened a back door and shoved me inside.

We were going to see the boss.

It was quiet in the car aside for the sound of Jermaine weeping. He was doing an amazing job of throwing them a false impression and producing real tears as part of the act. Beside him, Charlie's eyes were darting around like a chicken's as he barely kept his own panic under control. His feet were twitching, and his hands wouldn't stay still.

Behind us in the large car were three of the tattooed henchmen. Now that we were effectively trapped in the car and the doors were locked, their guns were away and they were facing forward, boring holes in the back of our heads.

It was Charlie that broke the silence. 'How are you so calm, Patricia?'

'Hey, no talking,' said the greasy little man in his cheap suit without bothering to turn around.

'This is not my first time being held at gun point,' I replied, ignoring the nasty man in the front seat. 'One gets used to it?' I replied facetiously.

'What do you mean it's not your first time? When else have you ever been held at gunpoint?'

This time the little man in the front swivelled to look at us. 'I said shut up. You talk again, I have you shot in the feet. I don't need you to be able to walk.'

Holding his gaze, I mimed zipping my mouth shut. Then I settled back into the chair and relaxed. The terror of being grabbed had passed and though I was still concerned about what would be waiting for us in Tokyo, I would use too much energy worrying about it now. I had Jermaine with me, and they were paying him no attention at all. Maybe all I needed to do was wait.

At some point, feeling spent from the burst of adrenalin, I drifted off to sleep, waking only when the car came to a halt. We were in a back alley somewhere, tall brick walls stretching high into the sky on either side and I realised I should have stayed awake and paid attention because now, if I managed to escape, I would have no idea which way to run.

The Zanooza began to bail out of the car on both sides, each with a weapon in hand except for the greasy little man who, once again, was smiling at us. 'This way,' he said, beckoning for us to follow as he chuckled to himself. 'Soon you will wish you had told me where you have hidden it.'

Charlie looked terrified and I actually felt sorry for him; he didn't deserve any of this. His mouth had to ruin it though. 'Why don't you just tell him so we can get out of here?' he hissed at me as we were propelled forward again.

Over my shoulder, I replied, 'Because I don't know what the heck they are talking about, dummy. I'm not in possession of whatever it is that they want.'

'You must be, Patricia. Otherwise, why would they want you?'

I didn't bother to answer. The little man reached the building to our right where two more Zanooza thugs stood guard outside. They bore the same tattoo on their necks to identify them as part of the gang and stood either side of a door which had an ornate version of the dragon tattoo painted on it.

Walking single file in front of Charlie with Jermaine bringing up the rear, we were led along a short corridor until we reached a large room. It was decorated with plush furniture, and expensive paintings adorned the walls. The doors were hand-carved wood of some kind, the carving itself yet another version of the same tattoo they all bore on their necks.

Coming into the room, I was the first to see the Zanooza boss. I was certain it was him from the position of dominance he commanded over everyone around him. Sitting in a chair that could best be described as a throne, he was naked from the waist up but had a black leather jacket thrown over his shoulders. I put his age at somewhere close to fifty; though his face bore very few lines, there was grey in his short-cropped hair and a pot belly that poked out from his open jacket to obscure his belt.

He started talking long before we got to him, looking directly at me for the most part but glancing at the greasy little man every few seconds as if waiting for him to report. The entire exchange was in Japanese, but the boss appeared angry though it did not appear to be directed at me.

The greasy little man looked embarrassed and cowed, backing away from the boss when the senior man ended his rebuke with a final comment and spat on the floor. Then he turned his attention to me and spoke once again in Japanese. By his shoulder was an attractive, slender woman in a sparkly dress that I hadn't even registered until she spoke, her words flowing as she translated what was being said into perfect English.

'Mr Tanaka requests that you hand over the lion's head now. It is precious to him and he apologises for the manner in which you have been treated. It was not his intention to scare or intimidate you. Mr Yoshimato overstepped his bounds in bringing you here at gunpoint and will be punished. If you wish to watch the punishment, that can be arranged. Mr Tanaka merely wishes to regain that which is rightfully his. You are, of course, free to go once you have surrendered the lion's head.'

As the woman fell silent, I gulped. I still had no idea what she was talking about. What was the lion's head they kept asking me for and why did they think I had it? 'I'm… I'm sorry,' I stuttered, trying to get my mouth to form words. 'I would gladly hand over what Mr Tanaka wants if I had it.'

The woman smiled and translated for me, her words coming out in the clipped bursts I associated with Japanese speech.

Mr Tanaka exploded, roaring his disbelief and pointing a finger at me as he gesticulated doing something unspeakable.

Once again, the attractive woman in the sparkly dress translated. 'Mr Tanaka urges you to reconsider your stance on this matter. He knows that you are lying because you said the word Anna and the number 2124. There is no way to know the number if you are not in possession of the lion's head. While the lion's head is notionally valuable, he wishes you to know that if you do not hand over what is his, he intends to flay the skin from your backs before boiling you in vinegar and will then make you eat your own kidneys.' She delivered the ultimatum in the same tone as a person reading a menu.

My mouth just hung open which Mr Tanaka took as a challenge. He shouted an order and the attractive woman took a step back as four Zanooza henchmen advanced upon us wielding cleavers. 'On your knees, please,' she requested politely.

'Patricia?' Charlie was all but gibbering in terror next to me. 'Patricia, what's happening?' I wasn't far from that point myself. Jermaine had yet to reveal his abilities, but he was one man in a room full of armed killers.

Searching the room for a ray of hope I opened my mouth to beg Mr Tanaka to believe me, but as I did, I caught the acrid scent of smoke. It caught in my throat and made me cough about half a second before the fire alarm started to blare.

The Zanooza henchman all paused, looking about in surprise as smoke began billowing in through the air conditioning grill set in the ceiling. The distraction was all Jermaine needed to get moving though. The three of us were halfway to the floor when the alarm sounded but while it took me a few seconds to reverse my direction, Jermaine leapt forward as if crouching somehow coiled his legs like springs. He struck the nearest thug with a high elbow and relieved him of his weapon.

Charlie screamed in confusion but leapt back out of the way as Jermaine felled the next thug to come at him. Mr Tanaka bellowed in rage but ran for a door in the wall behind his throne as he ordered his troops to deal with us.

The two remaining henchmen were bright enough to be wary, coming at Jermaine in tandem, one from each side to split his defences. It made little difference as he simply picked one and ran at him, jumping high into the air to deliver a roundhouse kick to the man's right ear and a straight boot to his chest as Jermaine's momentum carried him forward. The thug on the other side ran to follow after Jermaine, but merely ran into a large pair of shoes as Jermaine sprang off the ground and performed a back flip with a kick.

On the floor by my feet, the second thug to fall was starting to get up. He still had a cleaver in his hand. 'Arrgh!' screamed Charlie, near catatonic with shock as the man got his feet underneath him and started to stand up.

I hit him in the head with a fire extinguisher. The thug that is, not Charlie though I will admit I felt some temptation to accidentally hit my husband in the face with a large steel weapon. The thug elected to have another little sleep and the room was still again.

Except it wasn't. The pretty lady in the sparkly dress hadn't moved at any point in the preceding minute of violence. As the siren continued to wail and smoke filled the room, obscuring the ceiling lights, she slipped off her shoes and used a pen to wind around her hair and pin it in place.

She wanted to fight.

Jermaine looked at her with a frown of concern. 'I have no desire to cause you harm. I only wish to leave.'

Her answer was to squeal a banshee attack cry and leap at him. The nimble little minx was a skilled fighter, that much was instantly obvious as she broke through Jermaine's defences to strike his face and body and parry his blows as he attempted to force her back.

Charlie yelled, 'Let's go,' and grabbed my arm to drag me from the room. I wasn't going anywhere without Jermaine though. The fire extinguisher still hung from one hand so I lined up and threw it at the back of the woman's head. It flew true but she moved just as it should have cracked her skull, and its trajectory carried it on into Jermaine's chest where it bowled him over, the weight and surprise too much for his skills to defend.

I gasped as he fell over backward and again as she turned to advance on me. Charlie left me at that point, fear or self-preservation driving him to run to the door we came in through. It opened from the other side though and we were trapped in the smoke-filled room with the ninja chick from hell.

I backed away, bumping into Charlie as she walked nonchalantly toward us. She was breathing hard but so were we all as it was getting hard to breathe from the smoke still billowing into the room.

Beside me, Charlie shrieked again and I wondered what had caused it this time until I too felt the door opening behind us. More Zanooza were coming and the woman knew there was no chance of escape now.

'Are you coming or what, Patricia?' The woman's eyes flared in surprise and disappointment as Rick and Akamu peered around the edge of the half-open door. 'Dang, you might have overdone it on the fire, buddy,' Rick said as he started coughing.

I yelled, 'Get down!' as I saw the woman raise her fists again, but she had forgotten Jermaine and the fire extinguisher. It might not be an elegant weapon but when he bopped her on the skull with it, the effect was like an off switch being flipped.

'What an unpleasant lady,' he commented as he stepped over her inert form, dropping the extinguisher with a clang.

On the other side of the room, the door Mr Tanaka fled through reopened and two men with guns and gas masks appeared through it. They needed no more than a second to assess what was happening so we bundled through the door and slammed it shut in less time than that.

Bullets could be heard smacking into the carved wood panels as we ran away but the wood was too thick for them to penetrate.

'How did you find us?' My question was asked as we ran along the corridor as fast as we could go. The two old men had rescued us but were now holding up our escape as they shuffled along at a snail's pace.

It was Rick that answered, puffing slightly from the effort, 'We saw you leaving the caves. It was chance really; we were at the back of the group because we couldn't keep up and I turned around to sneeze and saw you. By the time we got back outside you were leaving in a big black car. So, we followed.'

'Followed? Followed how?'

Akamu looked a little sheepish when he said, 'We took a coach.'

Rick chipped in, 'It was lucky they didn't go fast because we wouldn't have been able to keep up, but we followed them all the way here and parked just around the corner,' he claimed proudly. 'We can use it to get back to the ship.'

Finally, we reached the end of the corridor and came out into the street again. The black cars were gone but I could see the coach parked at the junction where this street met the next. It was two hundred yards away but we could get there and escape.

Except we couldn't. As I took my first step toward the coach, a dozen Zanooza, led by Mr Tanaka himself, burst into the street from another door. They blocked the path between us and the coach, leaving us no option but to go the other way. They were way down the street, almost at the junction by the coach but it wouldn't take them long to close the distance.

Quick as a flash, Jermaine grabbed a big silver dumpster, pulling it from its position by the wall to form a shield between us and the Zanooza. Not a moment too soon either as the crack of bullets and the ping as they hit the steel shell of the dumpster erupted a heartbeat later.

Just like that, we were running again, Rick and Akamu yelling that we shouldn't wait for them even as Jermaine and I tried to drag them along. Charlie, unconcerned about the rest of us, raced to the corner and rounded it. 'They said to leave them,' he called back exasperated and I believe he genuinely intended to leave the two old men behind.

As Jermaine and I rounded the corner, I spotted our salvation; ten yards along the street was a bicycle rickshaw stand with several unattended rigs just waiting to be liberated. I pointed rather than shout, I had too little breath left to give instructions but Jermaine saw what I had in mind and darted forward to get a bike ready.

The Zanooza would be around the corner any second with a clear shot at all of us when they did. But we piled onto two bikes, Jermaine leaping into the saddle with Rick and Akamu barely on board as he started pedalling. And me? I found Charlie sitting in the big seat at the back of a bike he had managed to manoeuvre into the street but he expected me to operate it.

He even yelled, 'Hurry!' and gesticulated lest I dawdle. I honestly considered letting the Zanooza recapture us just to shut him up.

Jermaine's legs were pumping hard, his superior strength, fitness, youth and probably leg length propelling him away from me, so I was left in his wake. A shout from behind startled me, but it wasn't the Zanooza yet, it was the bicycle rickshaw owners spilling from the dispatch room to chase us down the street. One caught up to me and was yelling blue murder as he tried to grab the handlebars.

A bullet zinging by soon changed his mind and I glanced back to see a line of thugs chasing after us. They were grabbing the rickshaws and piling in to give pursuit. Those not pedalling were lining up their guns to shoot at me and I was certain our escape was about to be short lived when the sound of screeching tyres caught my attention.

Fearing a Zanooza driven SUV was about to run me off the road, I twisted my head to look behind and doing so meant I got to see the crash. Even Charlie, who had been hugging the seat and keeping his profile as low as possible, peered out to see what had happened.

It was Hideki's taxi! He had just wiped out most of the rickshaw-riding Zanooza by side swiping them and now he was barrelling along the street to catch up with me. In the passenger's seat next to him, I could see the shocked-looking face and blonde hair of Barbie.

I stopped pedalling and hit the brakes. We were saved!

As Hideki screeched to a halt beside my rickshaw, Barbie stuck her head out of the window. 'Quick, get in!'

'How on earth did you find us?' I asked, but as I sauntered across to the waiting taxi, feeling safe and somewhat jubilant, the sharp crack of another shot rang out.

In seconds, we were all in the car and it was burning rubber, fishtailing away as more bullets hit its back end. My door wasn't even shut and there were seven of us in a sedan made for five, but we made the next junction and held on to anything we could as Hideki two-wheeled it around the corner.

As he joined traffic flowing on a two-lane highway, Rick and Akamu fist-bumped and started cackling with laughter. 'That was friggin' great,' Rick snorted between laughs.

Akamu high-fived him. 'I feel like I'm twenty-five again. Man, I miss getting shot at.'

'Did you see their faces? Those crazy gangbangers, they got beaten by two old men, a butler, and an English lady. They'll never live it down.' Rick could barely get the words out he was laughing so hard.

'What about me?' asked Charlie.

Rick stared at him. 'What about you?'

'I was there too. You said they got beaten by two old men, a butler, and an English lady. What about me?'

Rick wiped the tears from his eyes as the mirth began to subside. 'I don't think running away counts for much. But you tell yourself you played a part if you want to.'

Charlie harrumphed but he couldn't go anywhere or do anything. Barbie had swung out of the way to let Jermaine get in the front and then climbed back in to sit on his lap which left Rick, Akamu, Charlie and me stuffed into the back seat. We were all kind of sitting on top of each other and it was getting hot.

I repeated my earlier question. Tapping Barbie on the arm to get her attention. 'How did you find us?'

Barbie reached out to place a slender hand on Hideki's shoulder. 'It was all him. He spotted Zanooza thugs outside the Aurelia and saw them set off tailing the coaches. He went to the security but they wouldn't listen to him. He kicked up quite a fuss and they called the police to arrest him, but he insisted they call for me because I could explain everything. That took a while, of course, so by the time I got outside and convinced the police to release him, the coaches were miles away. Even breaking the speed limits, when we got to Mount Fuji you were gone but so was one of the coaches and I remembered seeing it on the other side of the road, whizzing along with no one on board it. Hideki drove back here, and we searched the streets hoping to find some sign of you. He knows which areas are Zanooza territory so when we found the coach, we knew we were in the right place. Then I spotted Jermaine taking Rick and Akamu for a ride on the rickshaw and you know the rest.'

'What did those guys want anyway?' Akamu asked, though I could barely see his face with the press of bodies between us.

'The Zanooza boss wants something called a lion's head. It must be the thing that Riku Takahashi took and what they were going to kill him for. I told them I didn't have it but they were going to torture us to get it back and they would have done so if you two hadn't shown up.' I kissed Rick on his forehead since I could reach it and patted Akamu's leg because it was the only bit of him I could reach.

Rick said, 'Okay. But why would they think you have it? Better yet, how would they even know who you are?'

I had been thinking about that myself. 'They knew about things I said in Mrs Takahashi's house. They knew I had said the name Anna so my guess is they bugged the house after Riku took off. Whatever this lion's head thing is, they want it real bad.'

We were all silent for a moment until I broke the quiet again. 'I don't think the Brentnalls are involved.'

'Why is that?' Rick asked.

I took a second to frame my response. 'The Zanooza boss knew about 2124. He said that was how he knew I was lying. When I saw the number, I just assumed it was the couple staying in the cabin and... well, you've seen what they look like. I know I shouldn't judge, but they look like criminals. Now though I think I jumped to the wrong conclusion. Mr Tanaka couldn't know about a couple staying in a cabin on the Aurelia, surely.'

Akamu's voice appeared from somewhere behind Charlie's back. 'If it isn't referring to the cabin number, then what is it?'

Barbie chirped up from the front seat. 'Could it be a locker number? Like at a bus station or an airport?'

'It could,' I conceded but it felt too obvious.

'How about a zip code?' suggested Rick.

'Or an area code?' suggested Akamu.

'Who cares?' yelled Charlie, silencing everyone. 'Are you people all crazy? We got away. Nothing else matters now. All we have to do is get back to the ship and sail into the sunset leaving this godforsaken place behind us forever. This, Patricia, is precisely why I never wanted to travel anywhere further than England's great shores.'

He fell silent and for a few seconds nobody said anything. Then, as if he had never spoken, we all started talking as one again, all proposing ideas about what the number could mean if it wasn't a cabin number.

In the driver's seat Hideki said something. 'What was that?' I asked, not certain I had heard him correctly.

Everyone stopped talking for a second so we could hear him. 'It's a Hostess club. By the water on the north side of the docks. Popular place too.'

'By Hostess club you mean...'

'A stripper joint and lap dance bar. High quality place. I take lots of businessmen there. Power deals get brokered in strip bars.'

Barbie swung around on Jermaine's lap so she could see me, her eyes forming the question. I glanced at Rick and then Akamu. 'We've come this far,' the elderly islander said. 'It would be a shame not to finish the puzzle.'

'You have got to be kidding me,' moaned Charlie. 'We need to head back to the ship where it is safe. Doing anything else would just be stupid.'

Rick winked at me. 'Then I guess we're all just dummies. To the titty bar please, driver.'

I cringed at his choice of words, but I was excited again. Riku Takahashi had written 2124 on the note he gave me for a reason, and he begged me to save Anna. Mr Tanaka and the Zanooza knew who Anna was but I wasn't going to ask them to solve the riddle for me. I dearly hoped I never saw them again and I had to acknowledge that Charlie was right: going back to the ship right now probably was the sensible thing to do. It just wasn't what we were going to do.

The journey across Tokyo in the cramped car was mercifully short because the traffic was light. It was early afternoon, so kids were in school and workers were in their offices or other places of work. On the way we continued to discuss who Anna might be; the obvious answer being that she was one of the girls working at the club. We would find out soon enough. No one could come up with anything on the lion's head though.

It could be anything, but it certainly wasn't anything I had in my possession or had even knowingly seen. Charlie grumbled the whole way to the club, so when we arrived, the other six people in the cab, me included, wanted to get out so we could stop listening to him whine more than we wanted to escape the cramped space and oppressive heat.

Standing on the sidewalk, I looked at the front door of the club. A pair of neat doormen in suits were visible just inside, no doubt positioned there rather than outside because they liked the air-conditioning.

'Are you really going through with this nonsense?'

I turned to look at my husband. 'Yes, Charlie. I am.'

'Well, I'm not. I'm heading back to the ship and you are going to come with me and forget this ridiculous quest. The others can waste their time and risk their lives, but you are my wife and I say we are going to go somewhere safe.' I watched to see if he was going to stamp his foot.

Rick, Akamu, and the others were standing off to one side, keeping respectfully quiet while we had our domestic. There wasn't much to watch though. 'Hideki, do you know what the cover charge is?' I asked as I started across the road toward the doors.

A doorman swept the door open and gave me a congenial smile as I pulled out a credit card and led the rag-tag group inside. The second doorman opened a pair of thick black curtains to reveal the interior of the club. A heavy bass was pumping, and it was loud, but conversation would be just about possible if we shouted. The room was poorly lit, a deliberate tactic no doubt for all the dirty deeds that undoubtedly went on. A raised stage/catwalk dominated the room. On it I could see three skinny girls, all aged somewhere around twenty, all in their underwear and gyrating to the beat as men in suits heckled them.

It was a disgusting sight that made me feel sad for the men involved more than the girls. How pathetic were they that this was a good thing to spend their money on? I wasted no time on wondering how many of the clients were married with kids. Instead, I looked about for a door that would take me backstage; I wanted to talk to the girls and for that I would need Barbie and Hideki.

Next to me, Rick was leaning on the low wall of a booth. 'I'm not sure how much of this my ticker can take, love,' he murmured through laboured breaths. 'I haven't seen the like in years.' In case there was any doubt what he was referring to he flicked his eyes to the bouncing boobies on the stage ahead.

'Nor I,' echoed Akamu.

'Nor I,' added Charlie who had decided to join us after all. When he said it though, the same words were delivered with a definite barb attached.

'I need to get backstage,' I yelled over the din of the music. 'If Anna works here or used to work here, there must be someone who knows her.'

We hadn't gone more than a couple of steps through the black curtains, so when they parted again to let the next clients in, the first thing they saw was me. Unfortunately for the pair of young men now joining us, I knew them. Not by name, but they were two young guys from the ship's security team in plain clothes and out to enjoy the sights and sounds of Tokyo.

Barbie saw them too. 'Frank! Herbert! What are you doing in a place like this?' Caught like criminals in a spotlight, the two men, who until a second ago looked excited and happy, were now turning red and backing away. 'Shame on you!' Barbie yelled at their backs as they vanished back through the curtain. I shot her a single raised eyebrow at which she smiled and shrugged. 'That was fun. They will turn red every time they see me for months now.'

'Gentlemen, you should make yourselves comfortable and get a drink or something. I don't know how long this will take.' Rick and Akamu allowed Jermaine, who was the only man among them to be utterly unflustered by his surroundings, to escort them to a booth. I call it a booth, but it was a wide curve rather than an enclosed box and there was no table. Drinks went on small shelves just above waist height set into the back of the curving seat. In the next booth, a girl who appeared to have nothing on at all was kneeling over a sweaty guy in a suit as she gave him a lap dance. He was sitting on his hands so he wouldn't be tempted to touch her, and he was panting, actually panting like a dog.

Until he spotted me staring at him. My top lip was curled in disgust, as was Barbie's, I noticed, right next to me. He looked back at the naked body grinding away on his lap but kept cutting his eyes to the side to see if the two women were still watching.

With a grumpy noise, Charlie slid into the booth. 'I'm not paying for any drinks in here. These places always charge twice the price of a normal bar.'

'Oh, do they?'

Seeing his error, he tried to backtrack. 'Err… yeah. That's what I've heard. I'll have tap water,' he said as a young waitress, also in her underwear, came to the table.

I just rolled my eyes and shouted for Hideki to come with me. Leaving the guys at the booth, Barbie, Hideki and I crossed the room, walked around the stage and tried to go through the door that led backstage. It was locked though, our forward motion causing the three of us to bump into each other as we abruptly stopped.

'Is there another door?' Barbie asked, looking around for one.

A man who was not Hideki spoke. I couldn't understand a word of Japanese but it came behind me and sounded like a question. I turned to see who it was, to find Hideki was already speaking to the man. He wore a charcoal grey, hand-cut wool suit and a silk tie. I put his age at somewhere around sixty, but he was very well-groomed and had looked after himself.

Hideki turned his head slightly so he could shout to me above the music. 'This is the owner. He wants to know if the blonde girl is here to audition. He said we are late because the auditions were this morning, but in light of how she looks, he will make an exception and see her now.' The man in the suit was eyeing Barbie up and down, critically examining her like a buyer at a cattle market. Had it been me, I would have felt unnerved, but Barbie also heard what Hideki said and was playing along, slowly turning so the man could inspect her. His eyes and expression were not lecherous, merely appraising. 'He thinks you're her manager,' Hideki added.

If I wanted a way to get backstage, this was it. I nodded, smiled and stepped forward as I extended my hand. 'Hello. Yes, I am her agent. This is Barbie and as you can see, she will quickly become your headline act.

107

Especially once you have seen her dance. Can we go backstage to prepare?'

Hideki translated, his clipped sentences clearly pleasing to the man who nodded along and inclined his head in a salute for my directness. Then he glanced across the room to catch the eye of another man in a suit.

Where the owner was slight, the new man was burly though not nearly in the same proportions as the Zanooza thugs. I took him to be club security anyway but he came to the owner and bent down so his ear was level with the owner's mouth. Then, having nodded his understanding, he produced a set of keys from a pocket and opened the door.

The owner exchanged a few brief words with Hideki and walked away, leaving us with the burly bouncer. When none of us moved, the man in the suit gestured for us to go through the open door and shut it behind us, the noise level dropping significantly as he did.

Hideki pulled Barbie and me into a hasty huddle. 'Um, look, so, the owner is expecting Barbie on stage in fifteen minutes for her audition. She will be announced as a new dancer and given the chance to show what she can do. Or, um... what she's got.' Barbie followed Hideki's eyes down to her chest, understanding instantly what he meant.

'Why do I get the sense that you didn't translate everything?' I asked.

'Well, um...'

'Spit it out.'

Hideki's face flushed bright red as he stammered. 'He wants you to dance as well. He said you have a... um, nice rack.' Hideki was staring at the floor when he said it and flinched away when I moved my hand slightly as if he thought I was going to hit him. 'He has jobs for both of you and plans to market you as a mother and daughter act. He said you can make big bucks here.'

'Did he really?' I replied, searching for a response that suited the situation.

Hideki nodded vigorously, finding himself back on solid ground now the terrible news was delivered. 'As I understand it, the most popular girls in these places make a lot of money.' Then he saw my expression and clamped his lips shut.

The bouncer's expression suggested he was waiting for something. He didn't wait long though. We had paused just inside the door and were discussing our next move when he thought we should be getting on with the stripping. Using his body to make us move along, he stepped forward, giving instructions in Japanese as he did.

When Hideki looked embarrassed and didn't translate, I said, 'Let me guess; he's expecting us to get our clothes off now.'

'Uh-huh. That's what he said.'

We were being herded to a changing area where there were several other girls in various stages of undress. They were completely unfazed by the appearance of men while they were naked, which made sense, I suppose, but it was unnerving me. Barbie put her bag down on a handy dressing table, being careful to avoid a makeup spill and turned to me, shrugging. 'I suppose this makes me Lap Dance Barbie or something. I'm not sure that toy would make it into the shops though.' She blew out a breath. 'Might as well get it over with.' Then she turned so Hideki could unzip her dress. He glanced nervously at me, but Barbie was holding her hair out of the way and waiting, so he swallowed and did as he was expected. Her dress slid from her shoulders and she stepped out of it, grabbing a hanger from a nearby clothing rack to stop it from creasing.

Barbie, of course, was wearing a matching red bra and tiny thong beneath her red dress. Standing now in her underwear and red heels, she fitted in instantly with the other girls in the room, though I noted a few of them were looking at her figure with jealous eyes.

The only thing going through my mind right now, was what underwear I picked out this morning. I didn't remember. It wasn't something I put a lot of thought into, but I was certain it wasn't a matching bra and tiny thong.

To my left, one of the girls decided she'd had enough of the bouncer watching her and was now yelling at him and pointing to the door. The man merely shrugged, I guess he'd seen it all before a million times. He left though, heading for the door with an unhurried pace. Without turning around, he called out something over his shoulder as he went through the door.

'We have five minutes,' Hideki translated.

It was time to get on with it. 'Hideki, ask the girls if any of them know Anna or if one of them is Anna.'

He complied, listened to their responses and turned back to Barbie and me when he translated their answers. 'There is no one here by that name.'

'Ask them if there ever has been a woman called Anna here.' Once again, the cycle repeated but I didn't need to wait for his translation to know they all said there hadn't.

Barbie said, 'Maybe one of them knows Riku Takahashi.' Hideki tried that, but it was still a negative. Then three new girls came into the room just as two went out. They each had a sheen of perspiration on their skin from dancing; they were rotating off the stage as the next few girls took their turn. Just as I thought that, one more girl took a fast swig of water and hurried after the other two.

Hideki asked the new girls the same questions and I recognised Riku's name when Hideki said it. One of the girls reacted to the name, asking a question of her own.

'What did she say?' I asked, intrigued because we finally had a woman that looked like she might know something.

'She asked if we had a photograph.'

Crestfallen, because I had hoped we might uncover a lead here, I shook my head, but Barbie was fiddling with her phone. 'Is this him?' she asked, showing me the picture she found. 'He's on Facebook.' The photograph was of his head and shoulders and showed him in his crew uniform. It was very definitely the same man I had seen jump to his death just two days ago.

The woman recognised him when Barbie turned the screen for her to see, that much was obvious in her reaction. Excited, I asked, 'Does she know him?'

Her translated answer came back. 'No.' But as I let my shoulders slump in disappointment, he added, 'But she has seen him before.' The woman was still talking, Hideki translating as swiftly as he could though she wasn't pausing to let him speak very often. The story we got was that she worked as a croupier sometimes when she needed an extra shift. The tips at the gambling tables were nowhere near as good so she preferred to give lap dances. Fat American men who had been drinking were her favourite, but thankfully she didn't expand on what she did to gain their tips. She recognised the name more than the face, however she said he used to be a regular loser at the club, always betting hard on the wrong hands; the long-odds hands, and always getting further and further into debt. Some months ago, she couldn't remember precisely when, he vanished but there was a furore at the time which is why she remembered the name.

There was basically a man hunt for him. He stole something. She didn't know what; the girls working for the Zanooza soon learned not to ask questions. She did say that it had to be valuable though or they wouldn't have bothered with it. People that get into trouble with the Zanooza just vanish, which is what happened to Riku, but it was different with him because there was so much talk and rumour. She ended by telling us to stop looking for him because we wouldn't find him. The Zanooza would have found him and killed him at the time, retrieving whatever he took. No one ever got away from the Zanooza.

Except Riku did. He managed to get a job on the Aurelia and escaped to sea. Why hadn't he got off somewhere though? The ship had been around the world. Why stay on until it came back to Tokyo? He clearly believed the Zanooza were waiting for him, that was why he jumped. I learned something useful though: he stole from Mr Tanaka. The lion's head was something valuable and he still wanted it back.

I tapped Hideki on the arm. 'Ask her about the lions head.' She didn't know what that was, but she was telling Hideki something, speaking in animated terms before dodging around him to leave the room. 'What was that? Is she going to fetch something that will help us?'

Hideki looked a little embarrassed when he said, 'She needed to pee.'

Abruptly the bouncer appeared in the doorway, his eyes instantly bugging out at me.

'He wants to know why you are not ready to dance,' Hideki translated needlessly, the man's expression told me what he said.

'We've changed our minds,' I said firmly. 'We are leaving now.'

And just like I had with him, the man didn't need Hideki to translate. He stared at me for a moment, mirth tugging at the corner of his mouth and then he insisted – by taking out a gun. Barbie squeaked and backed away, but the gun was pointed at me; the bouncer's instructions easy to follow – take your clothes off, or else.

Cursing myself for getting into the situation, I unbuttoned my top, handing it to Barbie so she could hang it up, then popped the snap at the top of my skirt and stepped out of that as well. Now I was wearing nothing but bra and knickers, but looking down, I remembered that I had gone with the comfy ones that covered my bum – I had on granny pants. They were the fleshy colour people now call nude and my bra was white. There was a mirror just to my left but I steadfastly refused to look in that direction because I didn't want to see the roll of persistent fat sitting on top of my knickers or where the bra straps cut into the doughy extra flesh I have under my arms. Standing next to Barbie was part of the problem. Why couldn't I be in a line up with other women in their fifties? I might compare more favourably then, especially since I had lost two dress sizes recently. But no, I had to be two feet away from the world's most perfect woman, her taut midriff and rounded bottom the envy of supermodels. There wasn't an ounce of excess fat on her anywhere and she looked strong; her arms and legs long and perfectly formed with toned muscle sitting beneath the surface so it showed as she moved around.

Dammit it all; I was going on stage at a strip club to dance in front of men, one of whom was my husband, two of whom were male friends and the last of whom was my butler. Would I ever live this down?

My hesitation resulted in another burst of demands from the bouncer, his voice raised as he became impatient. I had no option, so as Barbie and I trudged out of the changing room toward the curtain that led onto the stage, I told myself I was really living life now, experiencing new things and making memories. I even chuckled as I pushed through the curtain ahead of Barbie, forcing myself to feel brave as I gritted my teeth against the looks I was about to get. I just hoped no one laughed at the old lady on the stage.

No one laughed though. No one laughed because no one was there. I saw the empty seats as soon as I got through the curtain and pretty much skidded to a halt. Barbie bumped into me as she came through the curtain.

Music still played but the seats were all empty. Except one. Where Charlie and the others had been sitting, was the women in the sparkly dress from Mr Tanaka's headquarters. She was staring at me with barely contained contempt, but she didn't get up and didn't appear to be armed.

'Mr Tanaka wishes for you to return the lion's head now. Your friends will be his guests until you do so.' Her voice rang out through the room, loud enough for us to hear it above the noise of the music.

I raised my own voice so she would hear my reply. 'I still don't know what the lion's head is.'

'Then I suggest you work it out if you wish to see your friends again. They will not be harmed, and you will all be free to go once you have returned what is his.' I doubted that very much.

114

'Our ship leaves at eight o'clock tonight. I haven't enough time to work all this out,' I protested.

'That is not Mr Tanaka's problem. Maybe you should ask Mr Takahashi what he has done with it. You clearly know enough about it to be involved. You claim to know nothing about it but here you are at club 2124 where the lion's head originated.' The woman was relaxed and the inflection in her words nothing but calm – there was no emotion attached to them, only the certainty that I would do as commanded or suffer the consequences. She didn't know about Riku Takahshi's suicide though.

'Riku Takahashi is dead,' I told her. 'He jumped from the ship rather than return here to face the Zanooza. I don't have the lion's head and I have no way of working out what it is.'

The woman turned her face away from me for the first time, looking down slightly as she ran the new information through her head. When she looked back up, she said, 'That is unfortunate, but it changes nothing. I suggest you get dressed and act swiftly if you want to make it to your ship before it sails.'

Hideki appeared around the side of the stage, coming back through the door we originally used to access the behind stage area. The woman was talking into a phone and pausing to listen, to instructions I guessed, but Hideki translated quickly. 'She passed on the information about Riku Takahashi. They are calling off the search at the ship.'

She put the phone down and levelled her gaze at me once more. 'The lion's head. Find it and bring it to Mr Tanaka.'

'But I...' I didn't get to finish my protest though because she pulled out a gun from beneath the table and shot a hole in the stage by my feet.

Barbie and I both screamed and ran.

115

There was no second bullet to follow the first, but in panic we darted back through the curtain to escape and ran into the girl that knew Riku. I say ran into her, but we bowled her over. Barbie managed to stop, but the bullet had spurred me to move fast so I slammed into her and the pair of us pitched over to land on the Japanese stripper, the three of us sprawling on the cold concrete floor in a pile of near naked bodies.

Somewhere in the tangle, Barbie's bra came undone so when Hideki came across the empty stage to find us, he arrived in time to see Barbie juggling her boobs back into it. He looked suitably embarrassed though Barbie spared his blushes and turned around until she was covered again.

'We should get dressed and get out of here,' I pointed out, desperately trying to work out what our next move could be.

'Where are we going, Patty?' asked Barbie, sounding despondent. 'If you don't know what it is that they want, how do we find it?'

Acknowledging the question but offering no answer to it, I pushed the changing room door open and went inside, scooping my clothes off the rail so I could cover my bare flesh finally. As I stuffed my shirt tails into my skirt, my phone started ringing.

It was the captain's name displayed on my screen. I snatched it up. 'Alistair?'

'Patricia, where are you? Are you okay?' He sounded concerned.

Telling him about my predicament was tempting. Right now I really wanted someone to rescue me, but involving the captain or members of the ship's security would only endanger them and what could they actually do? They had no jurisdiction once they were off the ship and Mr Tanaka might consider it a threat if I turned up somewhere with them. I didn't like it, but I had Barbie and Hideki and that was all the help I was going to get. 'Why do you ask?' I figured answering with a question of my own would distract him.

'There have been men here asking for you by name. They looked like criminals so we called the police and a stand-off occurred because the police wouldn't leave, the men wouldn't leave and no one was committing a crime or trespassing so the police couldn't do anything. Then I heard a report that you had gone missing from the trip to Mount Fuji. A search party couldn't find you or your husband or Special Rating Clarke and then one of the coaches turned up in a shady part of Tokyo. Do you know anything about this?'

'I might,' I replied tentatively. 'Alistair, what time does the Aurelia leave tonight?'

'Eight o'clock sharp. Hold on… why are you asking me that? Are you mixed up in something again?' I could hear his temperature rising.

Rather than answer, I said, 'I might not get back in time…' I searched for the right words. I didn't know what they were though because I didn't know what I was supposed to feel. My world was still so upside down. Alistair was clearly interested in me, I couldn't work out why, but he was. And I was flattered and almost embarrassed by his attention, limited though it was because of his position and work schedule. Other than formal occasions, such as the captain's table dinners, all we had done was share a bite to eat in my suite and have cocktails together, but I sensed there was more if I wanted it and that was the bit that confused me.

What did I want?

The concept of a relationship with a new man was throwing me completely off balance. I hadn't slept with anyone other than Charlie since I was a teenager, not that I was about to leap on top of the captain, but one thing would inevitably lead to another, so if I could consider kissing him, then I could consider what might come next. It was too confusing though, especially with Charlie here and now Charlie was in trouble and I had to save him along with my friends and...

I gave up. It was making my head hurt just to think about it. 'I might not be back in time,' I repeated. 'Will it be possible to catch up at the next port?'

'Patricia, what on earth do you mean? Please tell me what is going on so I can help.' The concern in his voice made my voice catch in my throat.

'Just hold on as long as you can. If I can make it back before you sail, I will.' Then, before he could speak again, I said, 'Take care,' and hung up.

Barbie was dressed and looking at me expectantly. Hideki was next to her, the same ready expression on his face. Once again, it was down to me to take charge. The girl that knew Riku was still in the changing room. She didn't know the club had been emptied because she was putting on a saucy nurse outfit that consisted of roughly the same amount of material one found in a tissue.

'Hideki, she said she didn't know what the lion's head is. Ask her who might know, please.' While he did that, I checked my watch. It was just after three o'clock. Leaving us less than five hours to work out what we were looking for, find it and get back to Mr Tanaka.

Hideki was listening to her answer, nodding and making mental notes. 'She says her friend, Emiko, might know. She dates one of the Zanooza thugs and, if her memory serves her correctly, he was one of the men charged with tracking Riku down when he went missing.'

'Can she take us to her? I can pay.' I was desperate and ready to clutch at any lead.

Hideki exchanged a few words and said, 'How much?'

'Whatever she wants,' I replied as I started toward the door. 'Tell her we are going now though and we have to hurry.' I had no idea where we were going and no idea if Mr Tanaka would even honour his promise to let us go, but I had to try.

Thankfully, Emiko, another stripper at the club, didn't live very far away. In fact, it turned out to be walking distance and for five minutes, we were outside enjoying the Tokyo sunshine as we followed Kaiya. We learned her name on route and more besides as she chatted animatedly, telling Hideki about her plans to study accountancy and give up the dancing before she got too old for it. I guess it was good that she had a plan, but I wasn't sure that lap dancing on men was the right way to pay for one's studies.

My deep concern that Emiko wouldn't be home, was relieved when she answered the door, Kaiya waving and hugging as she explained why she was on her doorstep with two Caucasian women. Inside, I got straight down to business.

'Ask her about the lion's head.' I delivered the request as if it was an order and Hideki was my employee to boss around. The ticking clock was affecting my manners but Hideki didn't react.

Emiko didn't answer my question right away though, she indicated for us to take a seat on a pair of sofas. There were five of us and only room for four bums so Hideki plonked himself next to Barbie on the arm of the couch as the two girls sat opposite us.

I had to bite my lip to stop myself from yelling for her to help me. She started talking before I got too excited, but it didn't sound like she was answering my question. When she paused to let Hideki translate, he said, 'Emiko asked how much you know about the movement of money in the Tokyo underworld.'

My eyebrows danced around a bit on my head as I tried to decide which expression I needed. Confusion won. 'What does that have to do

120

with anything? Please tell her this is urgent. I need to know what the lion's head is and how I find it. I don't have much time.'

Infuriatingly, Emiko smiled, understanding my tone if not my words and she started talking again. She talked for several minutes, Hideki asking her qualifying questions but making me wait for the translation. When I was just about to explode with frustration, she stopped and offered me another sweet smile. She had a bow in her hair and a round face that made her look like a humanised version of Hello Kitty. It was hard to imagine her taking her clothes off and shaking her goods for a living, but maybe her innocent features were the draw.

Hideki slumped back into the couch, a look on his face that told me that he, at least, finally understood what was going on. If he didn't start explaining it to me soon, I was going to grab his scrotum and make it touch the floor.

'Emiko says she doesn't know all the details and apologises if she has any of the story wrong.' I unclenched my fist as he started talking. 'She knows most of this because her boyfriend likes to tell her what he has been up to, so the account is third hand at best.'

'Just get on with it, please,' I begged.

'Okay,' he replied lifting his hands in defence. 'Riku lost a lot of money at the tables. He gambled away everything he had and plenty that he didn't have. He lost his wife in the process and borrowed more money from the Zanooza to gamble on long odds as he tried to win his money back. He lost even more though and the Zanooza pretty much owned him. He was taken to see Mr Tanaka but where others might have just been executed, Mr Tanaka gave him a task to perform. The story is that if he survived the task his debt would be wiped out.'

'What was the task?' asked Barbie. The room was deathly silent, Barbie and I enraptured to finally find out some details.

Hideki held up a finger. 'I'm getting to it. To stop Riku from running away, they took a hostage to ensure he came back.'

'Anna,' I breathed.

'Emiko doesn't know the name of the hostage, but this is the same tactic he used on you; taking that which is precious to the person involved. Assuming he took Anna, she is most likely still being held captive though I am unsure what he will do with her now that he knows Riku is dead.'

'Wait a minute though,' said Barbie. 'He didn't complete the task. He got on the Aurelia instead.'

'That's right,' agreed Hideki. 'His task was to take the lion's head to a rival gang, the Yakasi, where he would exchange it for something they have. Emiko doesn't know what that something is, but it must be something precious to Mr Tanaka or something of extreme value. When Riku ran away, it took them weeks to track him down, but once they knew he had escaped to sea, they sent Zanooza to each port on the Aurelia's path to recapture him. Emiko knows about this because her boyfriend went away several times. Each time though, Riku would come to the edge of the ship, look out through the exit and go back inside when he saw them waiting. They spotted him more than once and learned to hide out of sight, but he continued to frustrate them by staying on board, probably paranoid they were waiting for him. Which they were. Returning to Tokyo seven months later, the Zanooza were planning to board the ship in numbers and find him. I guess he anticipated that and that's why he jumped.'

I let the story filter through my brain. Most of it made sense now, though I had to worry for Anna, a poor woman that had been held captive for seven months now. Was she his girlfriend? She couldn't be a sister or another relative because Mrs Takahashi didn't know the name. There was a big piece of information still missing though. 'I still don't know what the lion's head is. Is that what he was sent to get?'

Hideki nodded that I had asked the right question. 'That is why Emiko asked what you knew about underworld finances. The gangs have some legitimate businesses that pay taxes and employ staff, but most of what they do to make money is entirely criminal. They generate huge amounts of money, mostly in the form of cash which they cannot put into a bank account or use to invest in the stock market for example. To move this money about, to account for it and pay for other criminal activities, they use a coupon system.'

'Coupons?' I repeated incredulously.

'Think about it. You can't carry the cash because there is so much of it and you are a criminal so you can't account for where the money originated from if you put it into a bank account. Not only that, you don't want to pay any taxes so you never declare any of it. A coupon system allows you to carry slips of paper of varying value that are accepted as cash within the criminal underworld and within the businesses that the criminal underworld control. Collecting protection money from a grocery store can be done using a coupon and the Zanooza can probably do their shopping using the same coupons.'

He was giving me an education in underworld finances but none of it meant anything. Seeing my expression, he jumped forward to the next bit. 'So, each coupon looks different to represent a different value.'

'Like the different presidents on the back of dollar bills,' chipped in Barbie.

'Exactly right,' replied Hideki. 'The lion's head is the most valuable.'

'How much is it worth?' I asked.

He took a moment to clarify the answer with Emiko before answering. 'Roughly one hundred million Yen... so that's about a million US dollars.'

'A million dollars. On a coupon,' I murmured. 'Does Emiko know what it was being exchanged for? No wait,' I interrupted quickly as another question came to me. 'Why couldn't Mr Tanaka just get another coupon? If he has so much money, surely he could just get another.'

Hideki nodded again. 'I asked the same question. The lion's head coupons are marked and issued in pairs. To retrieve the item from the Yakasi, only the correct coupon will do.'

Numbered. Startled by a glimpse of an idea, I grabbed my handbag and started rummaging for my purse. It couldn't be. It just couldn't, but as my fingers closed on the note Riku Takahashi pushed into my hand at the railings, I knew I was right. I had been carrying the lion's head around for the last two days and I had no idea.

With my face flushed in a mixture of embarrassment, relief and overwhelming euphoria, I held the coupon aloft. As I did so, I saw that the squiggle of lines on the back, which I had seen and ignored, was indeed a line drawing of a lion's head. I had been looking at it upside down.

I had the damned lion's head. Now I could give it to Mr Tanaka and I could get my friends and go home. Or could I? The niggling doubt that the word of a criminal gang's boss wasn't worth a damn resurfaced again.

Could I negotiate?

124

A Fresh Challenge

'You should go back to the ship, Barbie. There's no need for you to endanger yourself any further.' I said the words but I knew she wouldn't listen. I didn't want her to come with me but couldn't see any way to put her off if she was determined to come. It wasn't like I could outrun her.

She looked horrified at the suggestion. 'No way, Patty. They have Jermaine, and even if they didn't, there's no way I would let you go by yourself.' She took my hand. 'We've got lots of time. We can get the guys back and get back to the ship and in a few hours, we can be drinking cocktails and put all this behind us.'

It sounded like a wonderful scenario and I wanted to hit a fast forward button to get to that point. A ball of dread had formed in my stomach; we had to go back to the Zanooza stronghold to face Mr Tanaka. We had no choice but I couldn't believe he would just let us go. We had overpowered some of his goons only a few hours ago, set off smoke alarms in his building and injured people. The woman in the sparkly dress certainly looked like she wanted to get her own back.

'Do they have a number for Mr Tanaka?' I asked Hideki. But I got the untranslated answer when they both burst out laughing. Blowing out a resigned breath I asked him, 'Can you drop us off near the building with the dragon door?'

'Of course,' he nodded.

Still holding Barbie's hand, I started toward the door. With Hideki trailing after us, I said, 'I need to pay you for today, Hideki. You saved our lives for a start but your taxi now has bullet holes in it and you haven't taken any fares today because you have been ferrying us around.'

'It's nothing,' he started to say, but I cut him off.

'No, it's definitely something.' I wanted to give him money now because I wasn't sure there would be a chance to do so later.

No one said anything on the walk back to club 2124 where Hideki's cab was still waiting where he parked it. And no one said anything as we drove back across Tokyo to find the Zanooza headquarters. But as I reached for the door handle, Barbie squeezed my hand. 'Are we going to be alright, Patty?' she asked, a frightened tear in the corner of her right eye.

'You should stay here with Hideki, Barbie. You know how distracting men find you. I bet I'll be back out with all the guys in just a couple of minutes.' As I watched her face, she swallowed hard, then let go of my hand to grab her own door handle. We were going in together.

Ahead of us were two Zanooza thugs. I couldn't see any weapons on them, but I didn't think they would need them to kill Barbie and me if they decided to. They were standing in front of the door with the dragon motif but they stepped aside and pushed it open as we got to them, not that we got a smile or any sign of friendly encouragement, but we were expected it seemed and I wasn't sure if that was a good thing or very, very bad.

Inside the door was a man with a machine gun hanging around his neck, just like there had been earlier. Hidden from sight, I guess he was there to respond because the guys outside couldn't overtly carry weapons in public. He spoke into a radio while holding a hand up to stop us from going any further. My knees felt weak. We were inside the fortress of a criminal overlord and about to beg for the lives of our friends. My palm was sweaty against Barbie's but neither of us was letting the other go.

Time stretched out as we waited, the guard's arm up to keep us in place until a door opened further down the corridor and the greasy little man in the cheap suit appeared. He had a wicked smile for us but the first thing I noticed was the bandage around the pinky finger of his left hand. I had read about this, or perhaps seen it in a movie: he had cut off his digit in penance for his failings.

Mr Tanaka would have his lieutenants cut bits off their own bodies, but I was supposed to believe that he would let us go? My feet started pulling me back toward the door, but as soon as I turned my head to look that way, the guard moved to block it, lifting the muzzle of his gun to emphasise his intent.

We were going to see Mr Tanaka whether we liked it or not. Neither Barbie nor I spoke as we followed the greasy man along the corridor to the door with the intricate dragon carving. Passing through it, I glanced back to see the bullet holes in it from earlier. The carving on the inside was destroyed and I wondered if someone had been forced to cut off something to make up for it.

The layout of the room was much the same as earlier, but where we had been led into the room under guard last time, this time there were only two guards and they were both positioned behind Mr Tanaka. The woman in the sparkly dress was present again, looking none the worse for her fight with Jermaine and the fire extinguisher to the head. Her pleasant demeanour hadn't returned though.

'Do you have the lion's head?' she demanded as the greasy man led us to Mr Tanaka and stopped us six feet in front of him. Mr Tanaka was lazing in his throne once more, his chest and gut exposed again but he was listening keenly for our answer.

In response to her question, I put my hand in my handbag, a move which drew four weapons from different holsters as the two guards, sparkly dress and Mr Tanaka all whipped out their guns and pointed them at me. Barbie squealed in surprise and I swear a little bit of pee came out as I tried to stop myself from fainting in fright.

No one pulled their trigger though and I slowly eased my hand out to show them what I had: the coupon trapped between forefinger and thumb of my right hand. Sparkly dress issued an order without taking her eyes from me and the guard to her left crossed the room to pluck the ticket from my unresisting hand.

Mr Tanaka uncrossed his legs and sat forward, impatient to get his hands on the scrap of paper. He all but snatched it from the hands of his henchman. This was going well so far, by which I mean I hadn't fainted, and no one had killed us yet. Mr Tanaka inspected the coupon, turning it over and over for ten seconds or more but then a smile spread across his face and he started laughing.

He laughed hard and then he whooped and then laughed some more. Sparkly dress joined in and even the guards were chuckling because something was very funny, or perhaps because their boss might take offense and kill them if they didn't. It was infectious, so despite the terror of our situation, I too found I was beginning to smile. He seemed so happy; it was hard to not feel happy with him.

Then he spoke, a burst of clipped sentences that ended with an appreciative nod of his head in my direction. Sparkly dress translated. 'Mr Tanaka commends you for your efforts and thanks you for returning the lion's head. He says he feels it is unfortunate that you required such extreme methods of motivation to do what you should have done at the start. However, he is willing to overlook the damage you wrought today and will hold up his end of the bargain once your task is complete.' When she finished speaking, Mr Tanaka held out the coupon toward me.

Once my task is complete.

When I failed to move, he waved his hand insistently. He was trying to give me back the million-dollar coupon.

'What's going on, Patty?' asked Barbie though she knew I had no idea either.

I still hadn't moved, and Mr Tanaka's smile was gone. He was getting impatient and becoming animated, his raised voice shouting something at me.

'It is not wise to make Mr Tanaka wait,' advised sparkly dress.

With my eyes bugging out of my head, I hesitantly stepped forward, Barbie coming with me rather than let go of my hand. 'I don't understand,' I stammered. 'I thought he wanted the lion's head back.'

Sparkly dress quickly translated to Mr Tanaka, who looked at me incredulously, like he was looking at an idiot. When she translated his next words, my blood froze in my veins. 'No. Mr Tanaka wants what the lion's head represents. Riku Takahashi was supposed to exchange the lion's head for a package currently in the possession of the Yakasi. Since you have taken possession of the lion's head from Mr Takahashi, it is now your task to retrieve the package.'

'What? No, I...'

'Bring the package back to Mr Tanaka and your debt will be deemed to be repaid and you and your friends will all be freed.' She wasn't giving me a choice in the matter. I had thought the task was over and had harboured the hope that we would be allowed to go. Now a fresh level of hell was being heaped upon us.

'Why can't Mr Tanaka send someone else? Why can't some of his men go to retrieve the package?'

'Zanooza and Yakasi divided Tokyo into two parts many years ago. One does not cross into the others' territory for any reason. This is your task.

Complete it and you are free to go. Do not attempt to return to your ship though, we have men waiting there who will shoot you on sight. When you have the package bring it directly back to Mr Tanaka.'

Oh, my life. There was no way out of this. I had the stupid lion's head thing back in my hand like it was something sticky I just couldn't put down. 'What if the Yakasi kill me or decide not to let me go again once they have me?' She asked Mr Tanaka the question. He shrugged like it wasn't his problem. 'What about my friends? Will you let them go if the Yakasi do something to me?'

Sparkly dress didn't wait for Mr Tanaka's opinion this time, she answered the question herself. 'Mr Tanaka is a man of honour. Your friends will not be harmed and will remain as his guests until they are deemed to have paid their debt for today's... excitement,' she finished, choosing the last word carefully. Rick and Akamu had undoubtedly caused damage with their little fire stunt, Jermaine had taken out half a dozen of his henchmen and Charlie was just collateral damage caught up in it all just by being with me.

They were waiting for me to leave. The greasy man had already gone to the door with the wood carving and was holding it open for us to leave. I stared at the stupid coupon in my hand for a second, asking myself what they would do if I tore it into shreds and refused to comply. The answer was probably employ some ancient Japanese torture method that resulted in a painful death after many hours or days of torment so I chose to bite my lip and leave as I was expected to. However, as I started walking, I realised just how angry I felt. I was getting really fed up with being scared and even more so with being on the back foot and having to do what I was told.

With my blood beginning to boil, the greasy man leered at me and opened his mouth to say something as I went through the door. He didn't get to say anything though because I slapped him. I couldn't tell you why I did, it was an automatic reaction caused by frustration but something about his smug smile really got to me. Barbie gasped as the little man reeled backwards when my hard back-hand struck his face, but the non-thinking portion of me had sparked to life and my rising ire stopped me dead in my tracks even as Barbie was trying to tug me away.

As he sprang back upright, I knew he was going to bluster and threaten me. So, I stood my ground and faced him down. It helped that I was taller than him and heavier, but along the corridor, the guard with the machine gun burst out laughing and the greasy man threw himself at me in anger. I didn't move though which I think confused him because he was suddenly nose to nose with me and had nothing to say.

I held his gaze for another second, then turned and walked briskly toward the door. I was going to get my friends back and I wasn't sure I was going to play by the rules.

'Patty, what were you thinking?' Barbie asked. 'You are so scary when you get angry.' We were outside in the alleyway again, heading back to where we left Hideki. The same two thugs were positioned outside the door, both smoking cigarettes so we had to hold our breath as we walked through the fog of foul-smelling smoke.

I didn't answer her question though. I had too many ideas spinning around in my head to spare on anything else and I operated on autopilot until Barbie snapped me back to reality by squeezing my hand hard enough for the pain to register.

I stared at her. 'Are you okay, Patty?'

'Sure, yeah. I was... thinking.'

'You sure were. I had to ask that question four times and then crush your hand to get your attention.'

We reached the corner and what felt like relative safety, but Hideki and his cab were nowhere in sight. I paused to scan around for him, instantly seeing a car pull out of a line of parked cars on the other side of the street about two hundred yards up from where we stood. It was his car and as he drew closer, I could see that it was him at the wheel. My niggling concern that the Zanooza might be scanning for the taxi that ran them off the road earlier was unwarranted it seemed.

I was getting a feel for these hoodlums and I had a plan for them. Oh, boy, did I have a plan. I couldn't see all the moving parts yet, but it was daring and stupidly dangerous. Maybe it was even unnecessary, but when Hideki screeched to a halt at the kerb, I yanked the back door open and slid onto the back seat with a fresh determination that had been absent ever since Charlie showed up.

'Everything okay, ladies?' he asked tentatively because there should have been four men with us.

My brain still whirling, I asked a question instead of answering his. Time seemed too critical to waste. 'Do you know where the Yakasi territory begins?'

'The Yakasi? Why do you want to know that?'

'I'm going to pay them a little visit. I have an errand to run.'

His eyes were as wide as they could go when he glanced at me in his rear-view mirror. I left Barbie to explain what happened with Mr Tanaka though. I was still creating a plan in my head. The first thing I had to do was make a phone call, but I didn't want to do it with Barbie and Hideki listening. I had endangered my blonde friend long enough, so it was time to ditch her.

'Anyone hungry?' I asked. It was closer to dinner time than it was lunch, a meal that had simply never happened and my stomach cared not for my opinion about more pressing priorities; it was empty and demanded sustenance.

Barbie nodded glumly. 'I didn't want to bring it up. It seems selfish to eat when I don't know if the others are being fed or what condition they are being kept in.'

I, too, had the same thought; was Jermaine fretting because high tea at four o'clock would not happen? Were they in a cell, half naked and injured from rough handling when they were captured? Had they resisted and taken a beating? All these questions were stacking up in my head and threatening to overwhelm me. The uncertainty that they were even alive was driving me to make plans in my head as much as anything else.

'We need to eat,' I pointed out. 'You always tell me that our brains don't work the same when we are hungry.' I leaned forward to peer through the gap at Hideki in the driver's seat. 'We just need something quick. Can you find us a snack bar or something?'

'Sure,' he replied with a shrug. 'But I don't think visiting the Yakasi is a good idea. There has to be another way.'

I couldn't argue. 'Maybe there is. We just don't have time for it. Can you put the destination in the satnav? I want to see how long it will take to get there.'

Hideki was splitting his time between driving and looking for a suitable fast food place to stop. Now he added fiddling with the satnav to the list. 'The split is somewhere around Yokohama Highway, running northeast to southwest across the city. Once we cross that, most of the bars and clubs belong to the Yakasi. I don't know where their headquarters is, why would I? But if a person wanted to find them, all they would need to do is drive to a bar and ask nicely.' He was being flippant, but it was exactly what I intended to do.

The destination popped up on the screen showing that it was twenty minutes away if the satellite calculation was to be believed. I wasn't sure how much I trusted satnav and had never driven a car with one in it so I couldn't use it if I tried. That this one was in Japanese didn't help.

'Here's a place,' called Hideki from the front of the car as he pointed to a fast food place on the left. 'Will that do?' I looked where he pointed to spot familiar golden arches looming between buildings. 'You want me to hit the drive through?'

'No, let's stop and go in. You get better service inside and can check your order is right.' I said. 'Hey, Barbie, when did you last eat in one of these?'

She tilted her head to one side slightly as she tried to work it out. 'Like, fourth grade, maybe. It's been a while. I'll be putting in extra work in the gym tomorrow that's for sure.' It was good that she could focus on how to rid herself of the unnecessary calories. It meant she wasn't thinking about Jermaine and the gangsters for a few seconds.

Hideki slid into a parking spot and I had to be clever to enact the next part of my plan without arousing their suspicions. 'Can I wait in the car?' I asked, just as he killed the engine.

'Ah, sure,' Hideki replied. 'I better leave the engine running for the air-conditioning. It will get hot in here really quick if I don't.'

Barbie touched my arm. 'You want us to grab you some food, Patty?'

'Yes, please. Anything will do. And a coke,' I added quickly. Then I settled into the chair, making it look like exhaustion had caught up to me. They both bought it, leaving me in the car as they crossed the lot and went inside.

Quick as a flash, I got out and got back in only this time I was in the driving seat. Physically and metaphorically that is. It took seconds to familiarise myself with the controls and get the taxi into reverse; the steering wheels in Japan are on the same side as they are in England thankfully. I probably should have felt terrified that I was leaving them and heading off all by myself, but mostly I felt relief; they were abandoned, yes, but they were also out of danger.

Easing gingerly into traffic on unfamiliar roads and watching the satnav while hoping I wouldn't get lost, I put my phone on speaker and made a call. This was the part of the plan that terrified me most: I had no way of knowing in advance if the call would even be answered, but without the person at the other end, I couldn't hope to pull this off.

136

A red light stopped me, the driver in the car next to me giving me an odd look, not expecting to see a middle-aged white woman at the wheel of a Tokyo taxi. Then the phone stopped ringing as someone answered it, a gruff male voice starting to speak in Japanese.

Show time, Patricia.

'Hello, my name's Patricia Fisher and I would like you to take me to the headquarters of the Yakasi mob boss.' I delivered the line, practiced many times in my head, with an ironic smile and a vague hope that the two men I was looking at were in fact part of the Yakasi gang. They both looked like they might have joined the gang after passing some kind of initiation test where they had to eat a kitten or insult a nun or something. Their heads were shaved and much like the Zanooza thugs, their heads tiered directly into their shoulders as if necks were just so last year.

One man looked at the other, neither understanding English and I thought they were about to move me on, so I showed them the lion's head. It got their attention.

The satnav had led me through Tokyo, talking to me in Japanese which had been no help at all. However by continually glancing at the little screen and backtracking a couple of times to correct wrong turns, I arrived where Hideki had intended to go. The area was nicer than the Zanooza territory, which is to say that it was cleaner and there were fewer derelict buildings. It was still littered with bars that should have a warning above the door saying danger of death upon entry, and there were seedy strip bars and betting shops among the businesses I could see.

Battling my nerves yet again, I had forced myself to stop the taxi in front of a bar with two hoodlums standing guard outside and waved them over. Now one watched me while the other fetched someone from inside. Moments later, a silver haired lady with thick glasses hobbled out of the bar using a walking stick for support. She might have been the owner, a patron, or the thugs' mother, but she spoke English.

'This no tourist area. You go now.' Her English wasn't great, but it was a lot better than my Japanese.

'I have to exchange this for something the Yakasi boss is holding,' I said as I showed her the lion's head. Inside her thick glasses, her eyes flared in surprise at the coupon in my hand but in response, she slapped the nearest thug on the arm and babbled something I could not understand.

He went inside and came back out a few moments later, delivered an answer to the old lady and resumed his position by the door. Something was happening. I didn't know what, and it occurred to me that I couldn't be certain I had actually found the Yakasi. I decided to ask the nice old lady.

'Excuse me. This is Yakasi territory, yes?'

She eyed me like a fish on a hook. 'You stupid tourist. You get more than you bargained for,' she replied cackling as she walked away. Over her shoulder she said, 'You wait for car.'

I wasn't sure I heard her correctly or what I was supposed to do, but two minutes later, when I was beginning to question if I should ask again, a large black limousine eased to a halt in the street next to Hideki's taxi. Three large men in black suits, each holding a machine gun bailed out. Two levelled them at the car in a casual manner, which is to say they were not pointed directly at my head, rather they were in my general direction, but the action did the trick of almost making me wet my pants, nevertheless.

The third man opened the driver's door for me to get out. 'You will accompany us.' There were no other words of greeting or salutation and he didn't seem inclined to check me for a weapon. Silently cursing myself for being so brave earlier when I now felt utterly terrified again because I was here and alone and wondering if this was a huge mistake, I clambered from the car and closed it behind me.

Well-dressed thug number three hadn't offered his hand like a gentleman for me to get out of the car, but as soon as I was standing, he grabbed my forearm in a vicelike grip and yanked it so I stumbled after him.

'Hey! I came to you, there's no need to be rough.'

He heard me speak but paid me no attention, forcing me toward the open back door of the black limousine as his colleagues went back around to the other side. Thinking I should be thankful they didn't shove me in the boot, I found myself sandwiched between two of them on the back seat as the car pulled away.

Conversationally, I asked, 'Is it far?' My nervous mouth needing something to do. I got no reply, but as it turned out, it wasn't far to go; just around the corner in fact which explained how they got to me so quickly.

Where Mr Tanaka and the Zanooza had a mostly hidden door in the back of a building that largely looked abandoned, the Yakasi has a glass-fronted office block with the name of the gang emblazoned on the front in huge silver letters. I wanted to change my mind and run away, but the well-dressed thug with the machine gun had hold of my forearm again, dragging me across the building's lobby as his colleagues walked ahead of him to summon an elevator.

No one said anything, not even to each other, so though I wanted to babble and ask questions, I kept silent knowing they wouldn't answer me anyway. The elevator ascended for more than a minute, lights on the panel showing our progress all the way to the top floor where the doors finally opened.

By now, the ball of worry in my stomach was threatening revolt and I thought I might vomit if I had any food inside me. As the door opened

140

though, the thugs ushered me out but waiting for me was a pleasant looking woman in her early twenties. She wore a pin-striped cream business suit with powder blue Louboutin heels on her feet.

'Good afternoon. My name is Arida Sakamoso. I am Mr Tanaka's personal assistant.' She held out her hand to shake mine as the elevator doors swished shut behind me.

Confused by the change in attitude, I shook her hand. 'I'm Patricia Fisher. Did you say Mr Tanaka?'

'Yes. Mr Tanaka is the head of the Yakasi organisation. I believe you have something for him.' The woman hadn't moved and was clearly waiting for me to show her what I had so I fished in my handbag once more to produce the odd little coupon. 'Ah, yes,' she said, taking it from me to inspect it. 'Mr Tanaka will be disappointed.'

Disappointed? Oh, God. Was I in more trouble than I realised? 'Why? I asked. 'What does this mean?'

The young woman smiled at me as if something was funny and began walking toward the only door visible. 'Am I correct to assume you are just a courier?'

'Yes. Mr Tanaka... a different Mr Tanaka, has my friends and will not return them until I recover whatever it is that your Mr Tanaka is holding.'

Again the woman smiled, this time letting out a small laugh which she suppressed with a hand to her mouth. Then, as she opened the door and held it for me, she began to explain. 'The two Mr Tanaka's are brothers. They do not like each other very much and haven't spoken directly in many years.' The door took us into a corridor, which like the rest of the building, looked more like the national headquarters of a large firm than that of a criminal gang. 'They respect each other though and keep to their own territory. It is part of an agreement that goes back more than thirty years. They do, however, like to play tricks on each other. Finding little ways to bend the territory rules in an odd game they devised that only they seem to understand. The lion's head is part of that.'

'How so?' I asked, mystified that all the violence, shooting, kidnap and insanity could be part of an elaborate game.

We reached another door, which the young woman opened. 'I think it best if Mr Tanaka explain that himself.' Then, as she followed me in, she announced me.

Inside, the room was a large corner office with two walls that were floor to ceiling glass looking out from on high over the Tokyo skyline. Dominating the space was a desk with three computer monitors on it but to one side a table and chairs were arranged to suggest that impromptu meetings might take place when young executives visited with bright ideas. It was a power room and it gave no indication that the people in it were engaged in criminal activities.

Sitting at the desk, was a man who looked exactly like the Mr Tanaka I met earlier. His assistant said brothers, but she omitted to say they were twins. Despite the facial similarities they couldn't be less alike though. This Mr Tanaka wore a hand-cut suit of fine material, he was clean-shaven and looked like a model from an Armani clothing advert. Upon seeing me enter with his assistant, he pushed back his chair, stood up and crossed the room to greet me and shake my hand.

'Good afternoon. Thank you for coming. Can I offer you some refreshment? Water? Tea? Something stronger?' A vision of condensation on the side of an ice-cold gin and tonic flitted across my mind.

I forced it away. 'Just water, thank you.'

He nodded at Miss Sakamoso and as she scurried away to get my drink, he said, 'I am Ben Tanaka, I believe you have already met my brother.'

I nodded wistfully. 'Yes. I cannot say the experience was anything like this though.'

He chuckled. 'Yes, my brother does prefer to slum it.'

'Can I ask... this doesn't look like the headquarters of a criminal organisation, have I misunderstood something?'

He laughed. 'Mrs Fisher, where my brother likes to get his skin tattooed and wear clothing that tells the world he is a gangster, I prefer to present the world with the appearance of a legitimate business man.'

'But you are still involved in criminal operations? Because... you look like a lawyer.' I chose my words carefully, not wanting to upset a man I suspected might kill people on a regular basis.

'I have a degree in law from the Kyoto University but I can assure, Mrs Fisher, that all prostitution, gambling, drug trade, weapons trade and many other enterprises north of the Sobu Line are controlled by me. Now, I believe you have something for me. Something you wish to exchange for something I have.' I produced the lion's head yet again, handing it over as he held out his hand. 'Hmmm, I was finally beginning to believe he had given up and accepted defeat.' It was a cryptic statement that told me nothing. 'Forgive me, Mrs Fisher. You probably have no idea what this is all about.'

Miss Sakamoso brought me an elegant glass filled with water then retreated a few paces to wait for further instruction. Mr Tanaka said, 'Won't you please join me.' Indicating toward the table and chairs. 'Miss Sakamoso, can you please bring the package?'

Bewildered, I followed him and allowed him to pull out a seat for me. 'I have tried to negotiate a truce with my brother many times in the past. He refuses to entertain the concept and believes that he should run all of Tokyo. His methods are sloppy though; his tactics are overtly violent, and his business acumen and thus profit,' he said as he indicated about the room as a show of how well he had done, 'are a fraction of what they could be if he allowed me to run his half of the city. To prevent bloodshed, the two gangs do not cross into the other's territory and any that do are considered forfeit. However, my brother foolishly wagered that he could still convince me to surrender my half of the city by making my life too difficult. Not by attacking my business interests, but by targeting my family.'

I didn't like the direction this was going. Were there going to be children's lives at stake? Miss Sakamoso came back to the table with a white cardboard box. It was roughly six inches square with a lid that sat on top. She did not open it but passed it to Mr Tanaka.

'Over the years, we have played a great many tricks on one another. Using third party persons such as yourself to get around the territory rules. We have stolen children's lunches on their way to school, arranged subscriptions to services such as erectile dysfunction medicine or the Japanese over sixties caravan club.' I couldn't believe this. There were two crime bosses responsible for prostitution, murder, drug trafficking, and goodness knows what else and they played tricks on each other like a pair of infantile schoolboys. Mr Tanaka was getting to the bit about what was in the box though, taking the lid off as he began to explain the move that he thought had ended it all. 'In a stroke of genius, I sent a man to play chess with the father of my brother's wife. I knew him to be a boastful and skilled player, so recruited a man that would beat him, with ever-increasing wagers. Once he had him on the hook and in enough debt that it would cause a problem at home, my man offered it all back for one more game – but the wager was his wife's false teeth.' He finished the sentence with excitement gripping the timbre of his voice and tipped the box to show me the teeth. 'I hear my brother has been getting endless grief from his wife for more than a year. His mother in law got new teeth which he paid for but she doesn't like them and wants her old ones back.'

I sat back in my chair. Mr Tanaka had a beaming smile plastered on his face which he clearly couldn't control. He couldn't be happier – he was so proud of his achievement.

'So, you're telling me that Riku Takahashi, the man that was to bring the lion's head here to retrieve the teeth seven months ago, is dead; my husband, my butler and my friends are being held hostage; and I have been threatened, shot at and generally menaced for the last two days, because you were playing a practical joke on your brother?'

'Yes!' he exclaimed gleefully, either ignoring or not sensing the irony in my question. I wanted to punch him in his perfect teeth.

Trying to keep my tone even, I said, 'I hope you'll forgive me if I do not share in your joy.'

'It's just some harmless fun,' he protested.

'A man is dead.'

'Because he chose to kill himself. That was not of my doing. Nor that of my brother.' I could hear the mirth diminishing and sensed displeasure as he said, 'I think it is time you returned the package to my brother, Mrs Fisher. I have taken up enough of your day.' I had argued a little too much, the non-threatening surroundings making me forget the man opposite is a master of organised crime. 'Miss Sakamoso will escort you back to reception. If you need a lift somewhere, she will arrange it.' Then he stood up, pushing back his chair and coming around the table to shake my hand

145

again. I was dismissed but I had the package and maybe this was nearly over now.

'Mr Tanaka, before I go, may I ask one final question?' He met me with his eyes, waiting for the question. 'Will your brother really let my friends and me leave unharmed?'

'I believe so. It is in the rules that we cannot kill any of the pawns we use for our game. He is, however, far more erratic than he used to be, so… who can say?'

Terrific.

I had what I needed and a chance to escape, so I thanked Mr Tanaka, bowed my head nervously in return to his bow and got out of the room. In the elevator, Miss Sakamoso remained silent while next to her, my brain spun at warp speed. Did I have enough information? Had Mr Tanaka said enough? What would happen now? Reaching into my bag to check the time on my phone, I saw a dozen missed calls from Barbie and several text messages begging me to come back and not go alone. I ignored them all and put the phone away, noting that I only had two hours left to get to the ship and would use up another half an hour getting back to the Zanooza hideout.

I was going to cut it close.

The End of it

I politely declined the offer of a lift back to Hideki's taxi, remembering how roughly I was treated earlier. Miss Sakamoso was kind enough to point me in the right direction though, so a speed walk got me back to the car in a little under five minutes.

Except it didn't because the car wasn't there. It had been stolen. I still had the keys in my bag. Standing in the road, in the spot the car had been and cursing the sky, I almost died when a horn beeped loudly a few feet away.

'Patty, get in, let's go!' yelled Barbie. She and Hideki were in his taxi, both shaking their heads at me and looking annoyed.

I held up my hands in supplication as I jogged across the road and slid across the back seat. 'Sorry, guys. I didn't want to involve you.'

'Yes, Patty, we got that.' Barbie was being snippy with me. Not that I blamed her; I would be snippy too if she ditched me to go off and do something dangerous.

'How did you find me anyway?' I asked rather than dwell on the fact that I left them in a burger joint.

'I knew where you were going,' pointed out Hideki.

'Oh, yeah.'

'Hideki called one of the other cab drivers and got him to pick us up.' Barbie turned around to talk to me, her expression softening as she asked. 'Are you alright? How did it go?'

I explained about the Tanaka twins and about how nice the Yakasi headquarters were. I left out the bit about being bundled into the back of the black limousine but showed her the false teeth when I got to that part of the story.

'You've got to be kidding,' she said, staring into the box from the front seat.

'That's what I said.'

Hideki was trying to turn his head to see as well. 'All this is for some false teeth?'

'Apparently so. How far is it now? We are running out of time if we want to get back before the ship sails.'

Checking his clock, Hideki wriggled his nose and guessed. 'About fifteen minutes, if the traffic is kind.'

'And if it's not?' asked Barbie.

He shrugged. 'Tokyo is a big city. It gets snarled up at rush hour when all the firms in the city shut for the day.'

'Are you okay, Patty?' It was the second time Barbie asked the question inside two minutes, this time though she asked because I was fidgeting. There was something digging into me, both in the small of my back and in my bra, but it wasn't the sort of thing one should discuss so I dismissed the question and looked at my phone again. It had pinged an incoming text just as I got into the car.

The message was from Alistair, checking in on me and trying to confirm if I believed I would be back before the Aurelia sailed. He made no mention of the embarrassing situation last night but once again, he asked if there was anything he could do to assist me, expressing that he would put his resources at my disposal if I needed them.

My reply thanked him but declined his offer of help. I would love to have the ship's security detail turn up to rescue me from the Zanooza, but I had my own plan and it couldn't include an armed response.

Traffic, it turned out, decided that it would be kind to us, the journey taking seventeen minutes only because we got caught at more than a fair share of red lights. It had been moving though, which was unusual in Hideki's opinion.

As we neared the Zanooza base for the third time today, I broached the subject I knew Barbie would fight me on. 'I have to go in alone.'

'Not a chance,' she replied defiantly, the verbal equivalent of stamping her foot.

Nodding glumly at her, I said, 'I have to. And I can't tell you why. Not yet anyway.'

'What are you looking for?' she asked, picking up that I wasn't paying attention to her and was, instead, staring out of the window.

'Oh, err, nothing,' I lied. 'Just trying to memorise what Japan looks like. I very much doubt I will ever come back.'

'Nor will I,' she echoed. 'Or, at least, when the ship returns, I will not be getting off. So, Patty, why is it that you need to go in alone?'

I had one hand on the door handle ready to get out. 'Is it okay if I explain afterwards? It will make more sense then.'

'I don't like it.' Barbie looked glum. Japan had not been a great place to visit for any of us.

I replied with, 'I'll be as quick as I can.' Then I shut the car door behind me and walked down the alley to the door with the dragon on it. When I left here earlier, I was angry. Angry at being pushed around and at having no control over what happened to my friends. It made me do something which at the time seemed righteous, but right now felt risky and foolish. I was walking voluntarily into the lion's den and I was about to put my head in its mouth while simultaneously kicking it in the nuts.

I was expected, or perhaps just recognised, because yet again the pair of Zanooza thugs outside the dragon door pushed it open before I got to them. I didn't recognise them, they were different from the ones I had seen before, except for the tattoo on their necks that is. Just inside the door, was the usual third man with a machine gun ready to kill anyone the thugs outside took a dislike to. He actually smiled at me as I went through the door and headed along the corridor. I heard the static crackle of a radio behind me as the door guards called ahead.

The second door, the one with the wood carving, opened from the inside just as I reached it so my pace didn't have to slow as I went through it and back into Mr Tanaka's Zanooza lair. He actually looked pleased to see me this time. Leaning forward in his chair to see what I had for him.

He began jabbering in Japanese, though I had to wonder if he actually could speak English like his brother and simply chose not to. Sparkly dress had changed into a business suit and heels, but she was standing just behind and to the right of Mr Tanaka's throne just as she always was. 'Mr Tanaka asks if he can offer you refreshment,' she translated.

I nodded to acknowledge his kindness, but said, 'Please thank Mr Tanaka for his hospitality, but I am afraid I must decline. My ship leaves in one hour, so if it is possible to conclude our business, I would like to collect my friends and go.'

He waved me forward without waiting for sparkly dress to translate what I said. Did that mean he understood me? He wanted the box, that much was clear, so I took it to him, crossing the last few feet to place it in his hands. My heart was thumping in my chest.

I took a few steps back to keep a respectful distance, not that it would save me if he gave an order to kill; the room had half a dozen armed thugs in it. As I backed away, he pulled the lid open and looked inside. Then he looked back up at me. 'Well done, Mrs Fisher.' I guess that answered the question about his English ability. 'Was my brother in good health?'

The question caught me off guard. The evil overlord of the Tokyo underworld was showing concern for his estranged brother's well-being. 'Um, yes. He seemed very well.'

'Curse that man,' he spat. 'Won't he ever die?' And the character I expected resurfaced again. 'Did he brag about how he is winning the game?'

I sensed that this was my chance, my opening. I had to be clever now, but my legs were threatening to rebel, and I wanted to ask him to let everyone go so I could just run back to the ship. He deserved what was coming to him though and only I could deliver it, so I had to take my time and get it right. I licked my lips, my mouth feeling as dry as the desert, then manged to stammer, 'He was quite uncomplimentary actually.' I saw his eyes widen. 'Positively disparaging in fact.'

'You will tell me more,' he demanded.

'Well...' I drew the word out like I didn't want to say anything further. 'You might not like it.'

Suddenly, he was on his feet. He didn't advance but my feet took me back a pace anyway. 'You will tell me more, now!'

151

Quickly, I started to spill my guts. 'Ben claimed that your half of the city is being run into the ground and that your business practices are based on guesswork.' I was mixing truth with lies to draw him into talking. 'He told me your prostitution racket is barely making any money and that you have lost your drug trade to another gang without you even noticing.' Mr Tanaka's face was a mask of barely contained rage and veins were starting to appear on his forehead as his blood pressure boiled. 'He even claimed that you have lost your nerve and won't kill anymore which has lost you respect. He believes you will be overthrown by your own men very soon.'

'What?' he was incandescent with rage and about to go nuts. I would either get what I wanted, or he would kill me, and I was going to find out which it was in the next ten seconds. Staring right at me, he whipped a gun from behind his back where it must have been tucked into the back of his trousers. 'Lost the nerve to kill?' My heart stopped bothering to beat as we looked into each other's eyes for a second. My tactic hadn't worked; he was mad, but he was just going to kill me rather than tell me what I wanted to hear. His arm whipped out and he fired a single shot, the noise making me squeal in terror.

I wasn't hit though. Temporarily confused, I soon realised what had happened when the thug positioned behind me collapsed dead to the floor. He had shot one of his own men to prove a point and now he was spinning slowly on the spot, looking for any of his men to challenge him. He turned a full circle, stopping when he faced me again.

'I am the master of Tokyo,' he bragged. 'I have personally killed more than one hundred men and I have total control over my half of the city. My brother is an arrogant fool who wastes his money on plush surroundings and delusions of honesty while I embrace what I am. Prostitution netted twelve billion Yen last year all by itself: hardly a failing business. My drug trade will always be far stronger than his because I control the ports; it is nothing but jealousy on his part that drives his ridiculous claims. He will lose this game...'

Mr Tanaka continued to talk but I was no longer listening. The time had come for me to get out of the building if I could: I knew what was going to happen next. Waiting for the crime lord to finish speaking so I could ask to leave with my friends took longer than I wanted though. It was good that he continued to brag about his criminal accomplishments, but the clock was really ticking now. In the end, more than a minute later, he was interrupted by someone entering the room. A door opened in the wall behind his throne and the greasy little man came in. I noticed he now had two fingers bandaged, perhaps the second was punishment for letting me embarrass him. He spoke quietly to sparkly dress before retreating, sparing a hateful glance in my direction as he went.

The message was passed to Mr Tanaka, who considered it for a second before bursting out laughing. The message had to be a real hoot because he was doubled over and laughing so hard, he began to struggle for breath.

As the clock ticked down, I had to wait for him to finish laughing, though I did raise my hand to get his attention. In the end, I said, 'Excuse me.' Then, 'Excuse me,' again until he looked my way. 'I really must be going Mr Tanaka. Will you give me back my friends?' I wasn't going to beg. He was either going to do it or he wasn't, and I never really believed he would which was why I bought the insurance policy that would improve my odds of getting everyone out alive.

He waved a hand at a henchman though and collapsed, wiping his eyes, into his throne. 'Yes, Mrs Fisher. You can go. It would seem my brother has been arrested. The police managed to get someone inside his

153

headquarters with a wire and have a recording of him in which he confesses to several crimes. This is a good day indeed.'

'Mr Tanaka, there is one other thing.' He eyed me squarely, the meaning obvious: don't push your luck. 'I believe you are still holding Anna here. She was taken as collateral when you sent Riku Takahashi to collect the package from your brother, but Riku ran instead. You have no further use for her. Will you let me take her with me?'

I had reached the end of it; the end of the mystery. I still didn't really know who Anna was or what her relationship with Riku had been but if I could save her from this awful place then I would deem my self-appointed task complete.

He seemed to consider my request for a moment, but waved his hand again, 'Bring her out.' It was sparkly dress who went this time, going out through the door greasy man had used. Waiting for her and counting the seconds, I was extremely nervous. So much time had elapsed since I entered the building, but she returned less than ten seconds later.

She was alone though; there was no frightened woman with her, and my heart sank when I saw a basket in her hands. There was going to be a woman's head in it, I just knew it.

I was wrong though.

Sparkly dress came around the throne and held out the basket, my arms coming up to accept it instinctively. Terrified by what I might see, I caught a glimpse of movement. The basket had a blanket in it and something beneath it was moving. Then a corner of the fabric moved, and a nose poked out. Then an ear and two eyes as a tiny Dachshund looked up at me. On its collar was a pendant with a single word engraved: Anna.

A spontaneous grin tore across my face.

I looked up to say something to Mr Tanaka and that was when the clock ran out. The boom of an explosion rang out, instantly followed by machine gun fire and shouting. Dust filtered down from the ceiling as all hell broke loose.

Mr Tanaka, sparkly dress and the Zanooza thugs froze, but only for a brief moment before they all burst into action. As I ran to a large desk against the wall and dived under it to hide with Anna, they all went in the opposite direction and out of the room, heading through the ornately carved wooden door for the back exit.

They were no doubt wondering what was happening, but I knew: They were being raided by the police. I knew that without needing to see any uniforms because I set the whole thing up.

Crouched in the small space beneath the table, the wire I had in my bra dug into my flesh again. It was pinching my left boob and felt like it was cutting into me. The idea to take them down came to me just a few hours ago in club 2124 when I discovered they had taken Jermaine and Rick and Akamu. Oh, and Charlie, I suppose. At the time, I just wanted to give them a taste of their own medicine but in the hour or so after that, a plan with some merit began to form. I couldn't have known how well it would work or even if I could achieve anything worthwhile but when I made the phone call, everything slotted quickly into place.

I remembered that I knew only one Japanese person, Haruto Ikari, the former deputy captain of the Aurelia. I had his number in my phone and knew from Alistair that he was at home in Japan recovering from an injury sustained while trying to rescue me. I didn't know if he could help, but I had a vague memory of a conversation about his family in which he revealed that his elder brother was a Tokyo cop of some kind.

As it turned out, Mr Ikari was only too pleased to hear from me and very happy to make sure his brother not only called me but then came to find me in Tokyo. Kensei Ikari wasn't just a cop; he was the head of the strike force fighting organised crime in Tokyo.

Waiting for him to find me had eaten into the time I had, but he had come with all the bells and whistles, fitting me up with high-tech listening gear because they hadn't been able to pin anything on the Tanaka brothers despite years of trying. The Japanese gangs operated like a religion, looking after their gang members and using a strict code of silence whenever they were caught because they knew they would go to jail and be looked after by the other gang members.

Patricia Fisher represented a new player on the field but using the sports team analogy, the Zanooza and Yakasi saw me as the opponent's mascot. I wasn't on *their* team, but I also wasn't playing the game and could therefore be ignored.

Both gangs welcomed me in and bragged about their criminal activities, all the while being recorded by the Tokyo police. The only thing I insisted upon was a timed raid to get my friends back. All I had to do was goad Mr Tanaka into confessing to his various crimes and they would swoop.

So here I was, under a table with a sausage dog. I could hear shots being fired still, but none of it was coming from the direction the greasy man had gone; it was all coming from the other direction where Mr Tanaka, sparkly dress and the thugs had run. Could I risk going to look for Jermaine and the others?

I gauged that it was probably just as dangerous to stay where I was, so I slid the basket back out and into the open and clambered out after it.

Anna eyed me suspiciously. 'Don't worry, girl. We're getting out of here. Just as soon as I find my butler.'

Beyond the door greasy man went through, was a corridor, with lots of rooms coming off it to the left and right. I had no idea where the guys might be, so I cautiously tried a door. Inside I found an abandoned drug facility of some kind, which, from the look of it, had been vacated only in the minute or so since the raid commenced. I wasn't educated enough to know what I was looking at but if television can be believed, the tables in the room, set out with scales and little scoops was a cocaine factory churning out little bags of highly addictive narcotics. Along one wall were hundreds of Sake bottles though some of the bottles were on the tables which I thought curious, but I wasn't here to be concerned with drugs, I needed to find the guys and get moving. Kensei had promised me a police escort to the dock, but I would still need to rush even with blue lights leading us there.

I backed out of the room and continued on but there were no sounds of people on the ground floor, so when I reached stairs and could hear music coming from somewhere deeper inside the building, I figured I might as well keep looking. If the police hadn't come in yet, it had to be because they were still fighting the Zanooza outside. I could still hear bullets being exchanged and sirens blaring so it stood to reason that I couldn't leave yet even if I wanted to.

I started climbing the stairs, cooing to Anna that we would go soon, and I would find her a nice doggy biscuit to eat. This was to calm my nerves more than hers, a fact driven home when she yawned deeply and tucked herself back under the blanket.

The sound of music playing grew louder as I climbed the stairs and from behind me the sound of gunfire now appeared to be coming from inside the building to suggest that the police had broken through whatever hasty defences the Zanooza were able to erect.

My phone rang in my bag, or rather it vibrated because it was switched to silent for the meeting with Mr Tanaka. I also heard it vibrating about ten seconds before the first shots sounded, undoubtedly Barbie calling when she saw cops exiting their hiding places to converge on the Zanooza base. She caught me looking for them as we approached in Hideki's taxi, but whether she connected the dots to realise I was expecting the attack, I couldn't tell. Looking at my phone, I had three missed calls from her, but the most recent call at the top of the list was Alistair again. It was still vibrating, so I answered, 'Hello, Alistair. Are you calling to see if I am on my way back?'

'Good evening, Patricia. I...' his deep voice was calm but had stopped mid-sentence. 'Patricia, I can hear gunfire. Please tell me you are at a rifle range.'

'Um, yes, Alistair, that is precisely what you can hear. My friends are just about to take their last shots. How long do we have to get back to the ship?'

I heard him sigh. 'Patricia, the Aurelia must sail in fifty-two minutes. Are you far from the port?'

'Not far,' I lied, thinking it was at least half an hour in a car to get back, even with a police escort. 'I, ah... I had better go. Get this shooting thing wrapped up so we can get on our way, yes?'

'Please do, Patricia. I would be... together with your husband, you are the guests in the Windsor Suite. It would not do to leave without you.' He knew I was lying about what I was doing but now he was lying about his feelings. At least that was my belief. The start and the end of his sentence did not meet because he changed tack halfway through when he remembered I was a married woman. To him it no doubt meant his personal interest in me, which he was only just beginning to admit, had to stop.

Well stuff that.

'Alistair, I will be back on time, but if you have to sail without me, I will understand and will meet you at the next port.'

'The Aurelia sails at eight sharp,' he reminded me.

I disconnected and continued toward the music. Would I find someone inside whichever room it was coming from? Would they be friendly? That was a better question. I suddenly realised I was sneaking around the upper floor of a Japanese gang's lair with only a tiny Dachshund for protection and no idea where I was going. If I was holding hostages such as Jermaine and the other guys, I would place them in the basement in a makeshift, or perhaps purpose built, dungeon. Sensing the folly of my search, I turned to go back downstairs. Doing so meant I might not find the guys in time to get back to the ship, but it made more sense to find a hidey-hole to stay safe in until the police neutralised all the threat than to get shot now by a panicked Zanooza thug.

Then a raucous laugh ripped through the air and it sounded like Jermaine. Not that he laughed very often; it wasn't a butlery thing to do but it stopped me in my tracks and turned me around once more. The sound of music playing was coming from one of the rooms on the right. As I approached the door, there was more laughter and then I heard Charlie's voice, 'No! You took my queen, you swine!'

What the heck?'

I tried the door handle, startled to find the door unlocked, but as it swung open with me standing in the doorway, the scene inside took my breath away. Charlie, Rick, Akamu, and Jermaine were all partially dressed and were playing what looked like strip poker with half a dozen scantily clad hookers. They were also smoking cigars and drinking shots.

And they were having a great time!

I cleared my throat. Loudly. The noise causing Jermaine to look up as he laid a card. He had on black silk boxer shorts and his bow tie but nothing else except his socks and shoes. His socks were held up with suspenders. He saw my disbelieving, disapproving look and leapt to his feet.

Jermaine's sudden movement drew everyone's attention to him and then to me as they tracked where he was looking. All except Charlie who was next to lay a card and did so with a bellow. 'Hah! Now take off the bra, missy. Let's see the goods.' Only then did he look up, finally seeing me in the doorway with one eyebrow raised.

'Cards? I've mounted a rescue, nearly died several times, been manhandled, threatened and had to go all over Tokyo to solve this case, and you lot are playing cards with prostitutes and having the time of your life.' At least they had the decency to look embarrassed. 'The door wasn't even locked. Why didn't you try to escape?'

Rick raised his hand cautiously as if I might snap at him for daring to speak. 'Escape to where? Outside the door was a guard with a machine gun.' He peered around me to prove a point but then said, 'At least there was. They said we were Mr Tanaka's guests and would be held in a silken cage, which meant we would be well-treated and fed provided we didn't resist or try to escape.'

One of the hookers nudged another, her boobs jiggling inside her camisole top as she did. 'Uh-oh,' she tittered, clearly drunk. 'Mom's home.'

That did the trick. 'All of you. Get dressed and do it fast. The ship leaves in less than an hour.' I gave them about half a second to react, then shouted, 'Move!' as loudly as I could to jolt them into action.

Jermaine grabbed a pile of his neatly folded clothing, then because he had leaned forward to get it, staggered slightly and kept going, only stopping when he collided with a wall. He was drunk.

I face-palmed and kicked the wall. We were never going to make it to the Aurelia on time at this rate. Voices behind me in the corridor made me jump but when I turned, I saw police uniforms advancing, their tactical gear and weapons making them look dangerous but also comforting.

'Mrs Fisher,' a voice called from somewhere behind the advancing line of men. 'Mrs Fisher are you up here?'

It sounded like Kensei Ikari and it was, his face appearing at the top of the stairs and looking relieved to have found me. He came my way. 'Mrs Fisher, are you alright? Are you harmed at all?'

'No, Kensei, thank you. I am unharmed and I found my friends.' I pointed into the room, showing the senior policeman the half-naked and mostly inebriated men inside. Rick was struggling to get up from the floor and chose that moment to fart loudly from the effort. Jermaine, thankfully, was mostly dressed though he was having difficulty with his bow tie.

'Right,' said Kensei, taking in the scene quickly. 'You need to get back to the ship, do you not?'

'Yes, and we have very little time.'

Kensei barked orders at his men, several of whom let their weapons then hang from the strap around their shoulders as they went in to help the older men get dressed. 'I must thank you for what you did today, Mrs Fisher. We have been trying to infiltrate the Tanaka brothers for years, but they always catch our undercover men. After a while going undercover became recognised as a death sentence, so we stopped asking men to volunteer. Your offer to record them each confessing to their crimes was all I needed to have raids greenlit. This won't stop crime of course. The void left by the brothers will soon be filled and though we captured many of them today, there are many more Zanooza and Yakasi still on the streets. It sends a message though, today was a victory. You were very brave.'

I took the compliment with a nod. 'I had little choice. I thought they would kill us all once they had what they wanted.' Just then Charlie distracted me from what I was saying as he fell over trying to put his shoes on. I rolled my eyes and looked away. 'Had I known they were having such a good time, I would have just gone back to the ship and left them here.'

'Then I am glad you didn't know,' Kensei concluded.

The four drunken idiots were as dressed as they were going to get, and each had a strong policeman to guide them and help them along the corridor and down the stairs. Kensei led us to a different door than I had used before, one that opened to a street filled with flashing blue lights from dozens of police cars and tactical unit vehicles. It was dark already, my sense that too much time had elapsed confirmed when I checked the time on my phone. It was almost seven thirty. We would have to break the speed limits to make it now.

'Patricia!' Barbie called to me from behind the police barricade at the end of the street.

I grabbed Kensei's arm and pointed. 'She's with me. Her and the man next to her.' He spoke into a hand-held radio to get the barrier opened.

In front of me, the policemen were trying to very carefully fold Rick and Akamu into the back seat of a police car. 'Just shove them in,' I advised, aiming a kick at Charlie to get him moving but thinking better of it before it connected.

Hideki wound his taxi through the cop cars to pull up next to the one the guys were getting into. 'You're with me,' I told Charlie, grabbing his collar to steer him toward Hideki and Barbie.

'Oh, my gosh, Patty. Are you okay?' asked Barbie getting out to hug me in the street. 'When I saw the police raid swoop in, I panicked, but this was you, wasn't it? You called the police. That's why you wanted me out of the way. Oh, my God, is that a Dachshund?' One of Barbie's most endearing traits was how her brain bounced around between different thoughts when she got excited.

'I would like you to meet Anna,' I said, shuffling the basket a little so I could reach up to pull back the blanket a little more. The little red dog reacted to her name though and swung her head to look at Barbie.

'This is Anna?' she asked sounding stunned. 'Oh, my gosh, she is so cute.'

I smiled, but said, 'We have to get going. Can you give me a hand to get this wire off?' Putting the basket and dog on the back seat, I lifted my top to show her the tiny box taped to my back. Kensei stepped forward to collect it, looking away as I fiddled inside my bra to disconnect the microphone, and thanking me again as I slid into the car next to Charlie.

Then, as the door shut, Kensei shouted a command, rapped the roof of the lead car and we were moving, taking off at warp speed as we began a desperate race to get back before the ship sailed.

Kensei had given us all the resources he could, so with lead cars and chase cars blocking off junctions to clear our route, we sped across the city.

It wasn't going to make any difference though; constant glances at the clock on the car's dashboard told me we were not going to make it.

The police cars in front of us belted through another junction, closing on the port at breakneck speed but the clock now said seven-fifty-eight and we were too late. We would get there just as the Aurelia's stern churned out of the bay and would have to watch the passengers waving goodbye as the sun set on their Japanese odyssey. No doubt, for everyone else, this had been a wonderful and memory-filled two days exploring.

Despite my belief, I held onto a tiny ray of hope, but any chance we had of getting there was soon dashed as the police ran into a problem they couldn't just drive through: a train. The bullet train ran overland with the cars passing underneath, but the tunnels formed a bottleneck that backed up with traffic and there was no escape route the police could zip down because a truck had broken down in it.

Glumly, I accepted my fate. 'We can catch up with it at the next port,' I told Barbie, who was fretting in the front seat. I was sure it wasn't acceptable for crew to miss the boat, but I would square that away with the captain. Leaning my forehead against the glass of the window as I tried not to think about the drama and cost catching up to the ship would entail, I spotted a café across the street. From our position parked in traffic, I could see through the window to the people inside. In daylight, it would be impossible to make out what was going on but seeing it now I had to chuckle.

'What is it?' Barbie asked, swinging her head around to see what I was looking at.

'It's the owl café Rick and Akamu wanted to visit. I thought they were making it up.' Inside the café, patrons were clearly petting owls and feeding them as they enjoyed their evening meals.

Charlie had been silent since we left the Zanooza lair, but he chose now to make an announcement. 'I'm leaving you, Patricia.'

I frowned deeply as I turned my head to look at him. 'You're leaving me? Not the other way around?'

'The way you live your life now, the risks you take, the friends with whom you associate … I don't recognise you anymore. I'm going home. I have my passport in my pocket so I'm not even coming on the ship to collect my things.' I didn't think that would be a problem because I was convinced the ship had already sailed. None of us were getting our things. I couldn't work out why we were still trying to get there even, but ahead of us some of the cops had managed to move the truck and we were off again, picking up speed as Charlie took control and told me how it was going to be.

I didn't argue one little bit as he demanded a divorce and made it sound like it was his idea.

The last couple of miles was driven at the same extreme pace as those already completed, but as we came out from between the tall buildings, the tiny bit of remaining hope burst into utter joy as the Aurelia loomed large on the quayside.

It hadn't left!

'Yay! The Aurelia!' whooped Barbie, punching her fist into the air with jubilation.

I slumped back into my chair wondering what this meant as the gravity of the situation dawned on me. 'Oh, my. He waited.'

'Hmmm?' said Barbie, turning her head to look at me.

'The captain. He waited. The Aurelia is never late. That's what he always says. He held up the whole ship and all the people on board for me.' I felt stunned by the realisation. Ahead of us, the police cars screeched to a stop, their tyres leaving rubber on the tarmac. As Hideki also hit the brakes, the ship's security team were frantically waving us to hurry and get aboard. I placed my hand on Hideki's shoulder. 'I can never repay you for what you have done for us the last two days.

Next to me Charlie interrupted, 'Patricia, I am leaving.'

I paused what I was trying to say to Hideki to face him. 'Good, Charlie. Have a safe flight home. I will have Jermaine pack your suitcases and send them on to you from the next port.'

'That's it? You have nothing else to say to me?' he asked, sounding disappointed.

'Such as?'

'Patricia, this is your last chance to beg me to stay,' he said exasperated.

The car door opened from the outside, Lieutenant Baker doing his best to hurry us along. I looked around Charlie to smile at the smart crew member. 'Lieutenant Baker, so lovely to see you. My husband will not be joining me for the rest of the trip. Could you arrange one of the cruise line's town cars to take him to the airport, please?'

Charlie harrumphed loudly and pushed his way out of the car. 'I shall take a damned taxi, thank you, Patricia.' I think he would have slammed the door, but lieutenant Baker was holding it. He gave me one last angry look, then stormed across the quayside toward the line of taxis.

I breathed a mental sigh of relief and turned back to Hideki. 'Where was I? Oh, yes. I can never repay you for what you have done. I will try though. If I can arrange it, will you join us on a leg of the cruise soon?'

I could see he was surprised by the question. 'I, ah, I don't know. I have tuition and my job at the cab firm...'

'I will cover the cost of your tuition fees, Hideki. Whatever you have left to pay and whatever debt you have amassed will be paid off in full. You will be able to concentrate on your studies and not have to fit a job in around them.' Yes, I was spending a good chunk of the money I got from finding the sapphire but when I saw his face, I knew I was making the right decision. He had given freely to us, never once even raising the subject of his fare. Barbie was no doubt the greatest factor motivating him, but he had still done it.

Lieutenant Baker was getting agitated about getting us out of the car. 'Give me your email address,' I demanded, accepting a scrap of paper from Hideki as he quickly scribbled it. I smiled at the irony of returning to the ship with a scrap of paper, the very thing that had started the whole caper.

Barbie was looking at me, her breathing a little more rapid than normal and her eyes dilated. I knew why. 'Be quick,' I said as I slid from the car, accepting Lieutenant Baker's hand to gain my feet. Then, as he tried to lean in again, I handed him Anna and her basket to stop him. 'She needs a few seconds. That's all,' I whispered.

I risked one quick glance at the cab as I sauntered toward the royal suites entrance. Barbie and Hideki were locked at the lips. The chemistry between them, building over the last couple of days, had no time to be sated, but I told myself they would see each other soon enough if I got my way.

The awning at the royal suites entrance was already down, and the lines were being cast off as I stepped lightly onto the ship. The sound of running footsteps catching up to me preceded Barbie jumping onto the ship, just as two deck hands closed the door and made it watertight. Jermaine, Rick, and Akamu were all in the elevator waiting for Barbie and me, but the journey up wasn't conducted in silence as one might imagine. It was mostly a celebration.

'I can't believe we did that,' said Rick, a broad grin on his face. 'That was the most incredible two days of my life.'

Akamu nodded along, but he also had a wistful look. 'I just wish the girls had been here to see it.'

'Are you kidding me?' Rick asked. 'They would have ruined everything. With my Lisa tagging along, we would have had an itinerary and stuck to it rigidly.'

'Yeah. I suppose you're right.' Akamu smiled a conspirator's smile. 'What will we get up to at the next port?' Barbie and I both rolled our eyes at the same time and laughed about it. Then the lift pinged. 'I guess this is us,' said Akamu looking at the deck number. 'See you for breakfast?'

My two friends shuffled out of the elevator and the doors closed once more so it could continue to the top deck. A faint vibration told us the ship had started to churn the water, the captain no doubt getting the Aurelia out of the way to let the next great ship come into port.

As the elevator neared our deck, Jermaine shuffled his feet uncomfortably and cleared his throat so he could speak. 'I know you're going to apologise for getting drunk or something equally ridiculous, Jermaine, so just don't. Barbie and I love you just the way you are.'

'Madam, I feel I...'

'Shhh! Zippit. Nothing to be said. Understand?' I eyed him with a crooked eyebrow, daring him to argue.

'Very good, madam.'

The elevator pinged again, reaching its final destination at the top of the ship. My suite was just around the corner. 'You are coming for a cocktail, yes?' I asked Barbie.

'I want to meet Anna.' She cooed into the basket. 'I need to take some antihistamine before my eyes start itching, but yes, I am coming for a cocktail. I ate badly the last day or so and cannot excuse the dead calories in the alcohol. I think I need it though.'

The three of us all but skipped along the passageway to my suite.

I was home. That I came to think of it as home had a lot to do with not having another home to go to, but I was happier here than I thought I had ever been anywhere. However, when we rounded the corner and the door to my suite came into view, I saw the captain waiting outside for me and I realised what it was that I loved about the Aurelia: it made me feel hope. Hope for something better.

My pace quickened as we drew closer. His cap was under his left arm as he waited patiently for my return, but my focus was on his smile, his beautiful smile as he greeted me. 'Good evening, Mrs Fisher. I am glad you made it.' His eyes were not on me though, or on the small dog peering at him from the basket Jermaine carried, they were searching down the passageway. 'Your husband is not with you?' he asked, confused.

'No. Charlie is gone. He will not be coming back. We will be divorced in due course.' He absorbed the information without reacting.

Jermaine slipped behind me to open the suite door, taking Barbie inside to leave Alistair and I alone. 'Will you get a black mark for making the ship wait for me?' I asked, genuinely concerned but also touched that he would do that for me.

'Wait for you?' he asked, sounding confused. 'There was an issue in the engine room, Mrs Fisher. The ship cannot wait for a single guest even if she is the lady in the Windsor Suite. My log clearly records an anomalous reading on engine four. It would have been unacceptable to set sail until it was fully checked out.'

He smiled down at me, telling me everything I needed to know without admitting anything and right in that moment I knew what I wanted. Changes had been occurring over the last few weeks. Changes to me. Ever since I caught Charlie in bed with Maggie, my life, the person I was, had slowly faded away as a new version of myself emerged like a butterfly from a chrysalis. Today had been the starkest example of that. The old Patricia wouldn't have stolen Hideki's taxi and called the police to take down two different crime gangs. I felt strong and powerful and capable and more than that; I felt like I was just getting started.

I turned my head slightly as I looked up at Alistair's deep blue eyes, then, without warning, I stepped into his personal space, looped a hand around the back of his head and pulled him into a kiss. From my suite, I heard a suppressed, 'Whoop, whoop,' from Barbie as Jermaine tried to shush her, but Alistair didn't resist.

As I broke the kiss and looked back up at him, my top lip caught between my teeth as I thought about what I wanted to do next and a glow of excited satisfaction spread through me. I had wanted to do that for some time but hadn't even admitted it to myself.

'I... I must go, Patricia. I have duties to attend to,' the captain stammered.

'Of course, Alistair. I hope you will be able to join me for dinner very soon.'

He backed away a pace, but as he went, he winked. 'You can count on it.'

I watched him walk away, wondering if he had a happy jaunt to his step or if I was imagining it. Then, when he disappeared from sight around the next corner, I bumped the door fully open with my bottom as I backed into the room and turned to find Jermaine and Barbie staring at me with barely suppressed smiles on their faces.

'Shut up the pair of you and open the gin.'

The End

Almost

Epilogue

The couple in cabin 2124 slipped my mind completely until the following morning when I spotted them at breakfast. I met Rick and Akamu as agreed at La Trevita, an Italian place located in a wide atrium on the thirteenth floor. Anna and I had walked most of the way, the little dog growing on me quickly. Somehow, she was mine now and though I had never owned a dog before, I couldn't imagine surrendering her to anyone else.

She pulled excitedly against her lead, the sun coming through the large windows reflecting on her shaded red fur so that she almost appeared to be glowing. I scooped her up as I reached the edge of the restaurant's outdoor seating area, but as I took my seat, I spotted the Brentnalls at a nearby table. They were, of course completely innocent of any involvement in the death of Riku Takahashi. Their cabin number and the number written on the lion's head matching each other by pure coincidence. They didn't see me, which I thought was just as well since the only words we exchanged had been unpleasant. However, as I settled into my seat and turned my face to answer a question posed by Rick, I caught sight of something out of the corner of my eye.

Staring intently now at what I thought I could see, I said, 'Won't be a moment,' and got up again, offloading Anna onto Rick's lap as I walked around him.

'Where's she going now?' asked Akamu, his question aired loudly enough for me to understand I was keeping him from his breakfast.

'Damned if I know,' replied Rick. 'She's always up to something though. Hey, isn't that the nasty-looking couple we were following?'

Approaching the Brentnalls, Rick's voice faded into the background noise of the restaurant. I didn't think I could get close enough without them spotting me, so I didn't bother being surreptitious. Instead, I strolled right over to them. 'Good morning.'

They both looked up at the same time, though neither said anything immediately. They had eaten already, their plates pushed to one side with the remnants of breakfast still visible. Both had been on their phones, each ignoring the other as they conversed instead with an invisible friend or friends.

Edgar recognised me first. 'Hey, you're that crazy woman that stormed our cabin the other night. What the fruit do you want?'

Unpleasant as ever. I smiled sweetly in response and hoped he didn't use any more foul language as there were children present at a table just a few feet away. Erica still hadn't spoken but she had pushed her chair back and was eyeing me contemptuously.

I smiled at her as well. 'Yes, I wanted to speak to you about that. To apologise, of course. It was a case of mistaken identity. Terribly embarrassing.'

'I shouldn't worry too much about being embarrassed,' said Edgar, looking around instead of looking at me. 'You're one of those hoity-toity sorts staying in a suite, aren't you? Got more money than you know what to do with and think you can do what you like. That fella with you was dressed as a butler. I've seen them around the ship. He yours, is he?' Then he spotted what he was looking for and waved an arm frantically to get their attention.

I turned to see two members of the ship's security team walking toward us, one of whom was Anders Pippin, a delightful young man I knew well enough to address by his first name.

'Let's see if your butler can keep his job, shall we, Mrs Hoity-Toity? Crew are not allowed to touch passengers, that's rule one, that is.' Edgar stood up to his full height as the white uniformed guards approached. He towered over me, very deliberately moving into my personal space so he could impose his presence.

I didn't move.

'Mrs Fisher,' said Anders in greeting. 'Is everything okay?'

Edgar wasn't happy that he knew me by name. 'Of course. All the hob-knob rich rubbing shoulders together. One rule for us and one rule for them. Well, her butler assaulted me in my cabin, and I want him dealt with.'

The other security guard with Anders was a woman in her late twenties. She had bright ginger hair pinned in place beneath her hat and a Scottish accent when she spoke. 'That is a serious accusation, sir,' she said as she took out her notebook.

I'd had enough already. 'Yeah, I wouldn't worry too much about that. The bigger issue at stake is this.' In a single swift movement, I grabbed the bottle of sake out of Erica's open handbag.

'Hey, that's mine,' she complained, grabbing for it even as I yanked it out of her reach.

The female security guard eyed me with a stern expression and as Anders opened his mouth and began to speak, she held up her hand and shushed him. 'Madam, that does not belong to you. Please hand it back now.' She hit the *now* hard to emphasise it, but I didn't budge.

Both Erica and Edgar were looking worried, which told me my guess was on the money. 'This is not mine, right?'

'No, madam, I must insist you hand it back right now.'

'Because it belongs to this couple and not me?'

'Yes.'

Edgar said, 'Um...'

He didn't get the chance to claim that he had never seen it before because I dropped it, opening my hand so it fell to smash on the expensive-looking tiles. Liquid splashed onto my shoes but there in the debris was a clear plastic bag of cocaine. There were two more bottles in Erica's handbag.

From my table, Anna barked, her yip breaking the stunned silence that came after the smashing noise stilled every conversation in the room.

Anders spoke first as he murmured, 'Patricia Fisher does it again.'

The End (I mean it this time)

Patricia Fisher will return in Doctor Death.

Note from the Author:

Hi there, It's August as I write the end of this book and the summer has just been a blur. Our mostly sunny corner of England had been blessed with a heatwave that saw my three-year-old son retreat to his paddling pool every day for the last week. Like his mother, he seems to have sun-proof skin so just goes brown despite the factor fifty lotion slathered onto him and the pool's position in the shade cast by a giant cherry tree.

New chickens came to live with us a week ago, four replacements for two of the original chickens we recently lost. Trying to explain death to my son and what then happened to the chicken was surprisingly tough as he kept looking for them and asking where they were now. I am not looking forward to the day when we lose one of the Dachshunds. He plays with our little dogs every day and they follow him around like he is their pack leader. Fortunately, while they are not young, they are not old either and Dachshunds often live to twenty or more so I may be worrying about their inevitable prematurely.

The weather turned a few days ago, the first suggestions of Autumn making the days cooler and the rain is coming down outside right now, making me question whether I really want to cycle to work this morning. I probably will though, too many years in the army have resulted in a sort of sergeant major's voice at the back of my skull to insist I stop being weak whenever I consider the easier of two options.

Before I go, I should probably mention that this is not my first series; there are many other books already waiting for you. So, if you enjoy Patricia's adventures, you may wish to check out **Tempest Michaels**, **Amanda Harper** and **Jane Butterworth**. Like Patricia, they solve mysteries and their stories are written to make you laugh and keep you turning pages when you really ought to be going to sleep.

Finally, there is a **Patricia Fisher** story that you may not yet have found. It is part of this series but sits apart from it. It is called *Killer Cocktail* and you can have it for free. Just click the link below and tell me where to send it.

Yes! Send me my FREE Patricia Fisher story!

Extract from Doctor Death

Operation Fat Wallet

I watched from behind wide designer sunglasses, pretending to read a magazine as I surveyed the scene and tried to keep my impatience in check. Across from me, my good friends Akumu and Rick, two senior citizens from Hawaii, were laughing raucously as they told jokes and annoyed each other.

They were at the cabana bar next to the top deck open air pool where they were supposed to be acting a little drunk. The thing is, they weren't acting anymore. At least, I didn't think they were. We set up an hour ago, just the three of us on an unsanctioned and self-appointed mission to catch a pickpocket who had been plaguing the ship for the last week.

We are passengers aboard the Aurelia, Purple Star cruise line's finest and most luxurious ship, and I am the guest staying in the finest suite on the whole ship. Originally intended to house royals when they came aboard, I came to be the lady in the Windsor Suite by a quirk of fate brought on by a cruel blow that turned out to be the best thing that ever happened to me. I'm Patricia Fisher, one-time wife to a philandering git and now, somehow, I am travelling the world and while discovering myself, the tenacious woman hidden inside the bedraggled wife, I have also discovered that I am something of a sleuth.

Though I shook off my husband and have no companion with me, I am not alone; I have a butler appointed to me and have made several friends on board. Two of which are now my accomplices as we try to solve the pickpocket case before the onboard security team can. There is no reason for my involvement, other than because I want to solve the case and catch the thief. Rick and Akumu are retired police officers both enjoying the forgotten thrill of the chase.

179

Not that they will be giving chase to anyone; they are both well into their seventies and a little wobbly on their feet. Their top speed can best be described as a shuffle.

Anyway, the pickpocket has struck the bar/pool area several times in the last few days, generally picking on people with fat wallets or open handbags as they joyously pay too little attention to their belongings. That's where Rick and Akamu come in. They were drinking under the shade of the bar and making sure their wallets, bulging with notepaper not cash, were sticking out their back pockets for all to see.

Unfortunately, over an hour had slipped by and no one had tried to relieve them of their cash and cards yet. Safely tucked inside my magazine was my phone. Jermaine, my butler, had helped me construct an ingenious spy device so I could film the theft if it occurred while appearing to be doing nothing of the sort. Using cardboard, he reinforced the magazine to give it rigidity, then taped my phone in place so the lens looked out of the iris of the model on the front cover. It worked too. Glancing down at my magazine, I could see both men and the barman moving about behind them. The screen though was covered in dog snot, as the tiny Dachshund balanced on my lap kept nudging the screen with her nose, tracking my fingers as I zoomed and out.

'Anna,' I said impatiently for what must have been the fiftieth time in the last hour. She inverted her head to look up at me as if I was saying her name so I could feed her a treat. When we made eye contact, I said, 'Stop touching the screen. You are making it slimy.'

She tilted her head as if trying to make sense of my words, then licked her own nose and put her head back on my lap. I tried to dry the smears form the screen with the edge of my thin sarong.

Turning my attention back to the bar, a young couple had just collected drinks and were walking away again but had not gone near either man's wallet. Just then, Rick slapped Akamu on his meaty arm and slid from his stool. I couldn't hear what he was saying but it looked like the drinks had worked their way through his system, so he was off to visit the nearest amenities.

A pair of old ladies, each of whom had to be aged somewhere around seventy, made their way to the bar. The cruise attracted a lot of retirement aged travellers, possibly because they now had the time to indulge in the long trips or possibly because they recognised they wouldn't need to hang onto their money for much longer. Whichever the case, these two were typical passengers and I had seen them about once or twice but had not spoken to them. They were Caucasian, with silver hair though one had a blue rinse that contrasted with the pink cotton dress she wore to give a kind of bubble-gum effect.

As they came around Akamu, one wobbled slightly and bumped his arm, knocking his drink as he lifted it. I could see her apologising while laughing at herself, a hand to her chest to show her embarrassment.

Then, Anna growled, and I tracked her gaze to find, to my left, a shifty-looking man young man in a tracksuit and matching ballcap had appeared. Why would he be wearing a tracksuit? There was a slight breeze today which disguised the true heat, but it had to be close to one hundred degrees out of the shade. He bore all the hallmarks of a character to watch.

He was trying to look nonchalant but failing miserably, walking at an unnatural pace and looking nervous. He made a bee-line for the bar, but when he got there he didn't try to get to the bar itself, he just paused for a couple of seconds as he walked behind Akamu, peering over his head as if looking for someone and I saw his hands move in front of his body as he did something before moving on.

With his back to me, he had effectively blocked any chance I had of filming him commit the crime but as he moved away, Akamu's back pocket was starkly bereft of his wallet and the young man had increased his pace, heading across the sun deck area to the nearest door and escape.

'Stop!' I yelled as loudly as I could. A hundred heads turned in my direction as I pointed to the young man. 'Stop him. He just stole a wallet!'

Anna barked and leapt from my lap, her lead whipping through my hands before I could get a grip on it and she was off, sprinting across the sun deck at a speed that was frankly surprising for a dog with one-inch legs.

The man in the tracksuit and ballcap stared at her in disbelief, then started running. I was off my sun lounger but couldn't have caught the man even if I possessed superpowers. I didn't have to though. Anna was barking as she ran, attracting the attention of everyone on the sun deck; kids and parents alike standing up or standing on their loungers to see what was happening. Akamu was up and moving too, though I passed him and left him behind as I chased my little dog.

The thief in the tracksuit was going to get away though, he had too great of a head start and was moving too fast for even Anna to catch him before he got to the nearest door and could escape her. He put his arms out to push the doors open as he got to them but glanced back at Anna as he did, so he didn't see Rick operating the storm seal latches on the other side. Rick had heard the ruckus, seen the man running and me pointing and had taken an educated guess. The man hit the locked door at full speed, the effect much the same as running into a brick wall as he splatted against it and bounced off.

It didn't knock him out but it sure took the wind out of his sails. Dazed, he fell to the deck as a shocked gasp rippled around the crowd. The gasps, however, soon turned to cries of dismay as my untrained and disobedient dog caught up to him and bit hold of his arm.

Slipping in my elegant, expensive and completely impractical wedge-heeled shoes, there was nothing I could do to stop her. I was panicked that she might hurt him and then there would be questions raised about whether she was dangerous. I was just getting used to having her with me and she was so sweet, but my worries were unfounded.

The man in the tracksuit was sitting up again and had lifted his right arm into the air. Anna was hanging from it and shaking from side to side as she did her best to kill him by worrying the material of his sleeve. He uttered a few expletives and gave his arm a shake, his efforts succeeding only in making a nearby mother cover her child's ears in case he had anything else to say.

'Anna!' I shouted again, this time my voice causing the tiny dog to pause her efforts so she could peer at me even as she hung in mid-air.

Rick finally got the doors open again, but the commotion had drawn the attention of ship security so there were white uniforms converging on our location at speed and everyone on the sun deck was still watching us, their heads swinging about between me and the white uniforms and Mr Tracksuit and my overly aggressive dog and the old man stumbling out through the doors by the thief's feet.

Mr Tracksuit tried to get to his feet, looking around for his hat and acting a little dazed but he was quickly surrounded by security, their pace and youth getting them there at the exact same time as me.

'Put the dog down, sir,' instructed Lieutenant Baker, a tall, strong man I had come to know quite well during my time on board.

Mr Tracksuit looked up at him with a sneer. 'Put it down? Put it down? Are you kidding me? How about someone gets it off of me before I bash its head in?' I ducked between two uniforms to rescue Anna, clamping my hands around her muscular torso to pull her away though she refused to let go. Instead she continued to growl at the man and shake her head voilently. 'She's ripping the material now,' he whined, getting upset.

I lowered my head so my mouth was alongside her ear. 'Come along, Anna,' I begged. 'You're making me look bad.' In the end, with the security team waiting somewhat impatiently, Rick and Akamu swaying from the alcohol, and hundreds of onlookers craning their necks for a better view, I slid my finger into the back of her mouth and prised her jaw open. She contorted her body so she could lick my face, panting from the effort and looking ever so pleased with herself.

'Thank you,' the man said, not meaning a word of it. 'Now would someone like to tell me what is going on?'

With Anna secured under one arm, I stepped forward before Lieutenant Baker or anyone else had a chance to react. 'I'll tell you what's going on. You got caught, young man. Now, hand it over, please.'

Next to me, Lieutenant Baker sighed. 'Mrs Fisher, if I might take over now.' He shot me a pair of raised eyebrows as he waited for me to step back, saying, 'Thank you,' as I acknowledged that I didn't actually have any authority here. He opened his mouth the speak to Mr Tracksuit but paused and spoke to me first. 'I must say it is so unusual to find you in the thick of it, Mrs Fisher.' His flippant comment was delivered with a smile though I gave him an innocent face in response as if I had no idea what he was talking about.

'Hey!' said Mr Tracksuit, bringing everyone's attention back to him. 'How about someone tells me what is going on?'

This time Baker did address him, 'Sir, I must insist that you hand it over now, please.'

'Don't know what you're talking about,' insisted Mr Tracksuit.

Lieutenant Deepa Bhukari said, 'We saw you take this man's wallet.' She indicated Akamu. 'We need to escort you to a secure area for questioning and inspect your cabin for other property we believe you may have taken.'

'You didn't see me take anything,' he claimed defiantly. 'Search me. Go on. Search me,' he demanded as he lifted his arms to assume a classic pat-down pose. His confidence was worrying. Had he ditched the wallet? If so, where? I looked about to see if he had passed a trash can. His prints or DNA would be on the wallet if we found he had thrown it already. There was nothing in sight though.

Lieutenant Baker searched the man but as expected; he found nothing. He certainly didn't find Akamu's wallet.

Wrinkling my nose, I looked back at the bar. The two old ladies were no longer there. 'Lieutenant Baker, could I have a quiet word?'

He stepped to one side with me, away from the others who were still surrounding the man in the tracksuit. We were creating a scene; more than usual I mean and would have to move away soon.

As Baker stepped close to me so I could speak quietly, I ran it through in my head again: I was about to accuse a pair of pensioners. 'There was another couple near Akamu when his wallet went missing,' I said.

Baker eyed me in confusion for a second, then said, 'You don't mean the little old ladies, do you?'

'The kid gets to lift the wallet but then palms it to one of the ladies who totters away with it in her handbag. Perfect set up.'

'No way.'

Lieutenant Baker didn't like it, but I persisted. 'The wallet has gone, Mr Tracksuit doesn't have it, and he hasn't had a chance to put it anywhere. If the ladies didn't take it, then where is it?'

His shoulders slumped in defeat. 'Okay, Mrs Fisher. Let's take a look at the lovely little old ladies.' Then he turned to the other security members just a few feet away. 'Take him to holding, please. Identify him and wait there. Mrs Fisher and I will be along soon.'

Baker started to walk away, touching my elbow gently to get me moving also. 'Just the two of us?' I asked.

'I doubt our quarry will put up much of a fight. If it's them, I will call security to join me at their cabin.' Baker was moving swiftly, walking not running but not hanging about either. He had a question for me though, 'How is it that you came to be chasing him, Mrs Fisher? It feels like too much coincidence for it to be your friend whose wallet was taken.'

'We set a trap, okay,' I admitted, setting Anna down but keeping a good hold on her lead this time as she instantly started pulling against it. 'What were you doing there?'

'It's my job,' he drawled as if he shouldn't have to remind me. 'We also had a trap set up, but I guess yours was more attractive.'

We hit the doors to go inside on the opposite side of the sun deck from where we had been. 'Do you know where you are going?' I asked.

Baker pointed down the passageway ahead of us. 'Yes, I helped the old ladies with some bags yesterday.' He fell silent for a moment though it seemed like he wanted to say something else, so I kept quiet too. Just before we reached the next corner, he said, 'Of course, I'm now wondering if the bags were theirs because there have been reports of shopping going missing.'

'Shopping?'

'Clothes. Designer goods. Some of the shops on board sell expensive items that might be attractive to a thief. I think maybe I helped them carry stolen goods to their cabin.' He said it with a sigh but as we turned the corner, we both saw the old ladies ahead of us.

They were about to get in an elevator!

'Ladies, stop!' Baker shouted, drawing the attention of everyone in sight including the old ladies. Their eyes went wide with panic, but they didn't stop as instructed. Instead, they dashed inside the elevator car, bumping into each other as they did which caused items to spill from a handbag as they desperately stabbed the button to close the doors.

Baker and I were both running, little Anna's feet skidding on the deck as she attempted to break the sound barrier while I held her in check on her lead. The doors closed before we could get there though, the faces of the two ladies looking scared as they backed against the rear wall of the car and vanished from sight.

They escaped, but not for long. Baker knew their cabin number.

On the deck by our feet were two wallets. Anna was sniffing them. 'Am I okay to pick these up?' I asked, but Baker was already on his radio, coordinating a response that would meet him at the ladies' cabin. As he did that, I knelt on the deck and fished in my own handbag for a pen.

Using it, so I didn't get my fingerprints on the wallets, I flicked them both open. Neither was Akamu's.

The first showed a Fiji address on the drivers' license in the clear plastic picture bit inside. The man was broad with an unsmiling face as one always gets with such pictures, but his age was listed as sixty-two and we had his name so the crew would be able to return his property. The second one didn't have a drivers' licence displayed inside, instead it had what looked like the identification for a doctor of some kind. It looked to be in Filipino, though there was no address shown. Scanning the details, I saw Doktor written next to the word immunology. I was wiling to bet that immunology was the same word most places, so it meant exactly what I thought it meant.

'I need those, please,' said Baker, kneeling next to me to carefully scoop both wallets into two separate evidence bags using a plastic-gloved hand. 'I have a team meeting me at the ladies' cabin. It looks like another case closed.'

I went with him, though there was no need for me to do so. I like closure, I guess. Baker's confidence in closing the case was premature though because the ladies were not there when we arrived. However, the question of whether they were the thieves or not was answered unequivocally. The ladies had absconded to somewhere else on the ship and were no doubt hiding out and wondering what to do, but their cabin was filled with stolen goods. Wallets, pieces of jewellery, purses and handbags, shopping bags filled with the expensive, designer-labelled items Baker described were strewn across the bed and the chest of drawers and the dressing table and even stacked in the corners.

Lieutenant Bhukari whistled appreciatively. 'Wow. This is quite the haul. Does anyone know how long they have been on board?'

Lieutenant Pippin, another crew member I knew, answered, 'I am just looking that up now.'

Across the room, Baker was looking over the shoulders of two other men as they peered inside some of the bags. 'This is going to take a while to catalogue and return,' one said.

'We have a day,' replied Baker. 'When we dock in Kandarri tomorrow, some passengers will be getting off and we need to have their belongings returned to them.'

'You're kidding right?' the man said.

Baker eyed him curiously. 'It will take far longer if you bellyache instead of getting started.' His subordinate looked like he wanted to say something but chose instead to get on with it as suggested.

Anders spoke up to break the tension. 'The ladies got on in Singapore. They are Irish though. Their names are Agnes Eldritch and Mavis Du Maurier.' He looked up from the tablet in his hands. 'I suppose we need to circulate their pictures and find them.'

Bhukari asked, 'What do we do about the man we already took into custody?'

Baker pointed a finger at Pippin. 'Is he linked to the ladies?'

Pippin busied himself typing on the tablet, but said, 'I don't... no, not that I can see. They got on in different places, come from different countries and are staying on different decks.'

'Then we let him go and apologise,' concluded Baker. 'I'll do that myself. Pippin, get the pictures circulated to all crew and inform Commander Shriver. Bhukari, you take charge here and seal off the room.

189

I suggest you work quietly and with the door closed. If they cannot see anyone, the ladies may attempt to return and walk right in on top of you.'

I nodded at his plan. It was simple and might yield them an easy win. As Baker excused himself to deal with the man in the tracksuit, I realised I had no further purpose and was most likely in the way. I wasn't satisfied about Mr Tracksuit though. He had been wearing a sweat-inducing outfit in hundred-degree sunshine and there had to be a reason for that.

Checking to make sure no one was watching, I surreptitiously knocked the two wallets we found by the elevators into my handbag. Baker had placed them on the dressing table in their plastic evidence bags and they were still there, unguarded amid all the other detritus. I was going to return them, and there was more than enough evidence in the cabin to convict Agnes and Mavis, so it wasn't as if I was doing anything wrong. That's how I explained it to Anna at least.

I wanted to meet a couple of the victims; I had a few questions to ask.